The
SUNDAE
DELIVERY
SERVICE

A MESSAGE FROM CHICKEN HOUSE

I love being back with the charming – and a little odd – Orinthia and her family, along with the evergrowing menagerie of postal delivery animals. This time, they're embroiled in an ice cream mystery with high stakes! Holly Rivers writes a world of true wonder – funny, endearing, but with a backbone of kindness and mildly unexpected good sense. Come and join in! You'll love it too!

BARRY CUNNINGHAM
Publisher
Chicken House

HOLLY RIVERS

The SUNDAE DELIVERY SERVICE

Chicken House

2 PALMER STREET, FROME,
SOMERSET BA11 1DS

Text © Holly Rivers 2023
Illustrations © Rachael Dean 2023

First published in Great Britain in 2023
Chicken House
2 Palmer Street
Frome, Somerset BA11 1DS
United Kingdom
www.chickenhousebooks.com

Chicken House/Scholastic Ireland, 89E Lagan Road, Dublin Industrial Estate,
Glasnevin, Dublin D11 HP5F, Republic of Ireland

Cover and interior design by Steve Wells
Cover and interior illustration by Rachael Dean
Typeset by Dorchester Typesetting Group Ltd
Printed in Great Britain by Clays, Elcograf S.p.A

FSC
www.fsc.org
MIX
Paper | Supporting
responsible forestry
FSC® C018072

1 3 5 7 9 10 8 6 4 2

British Library Cataloguing in Publication data available.

PB ISBN 978-1-912626-05-2
eISBN 978-1-915026-75-0

For my parents, Toby and Siân.
I love you both with a cherry on top.

And for Courtney, who loved eating ice cream by the sea.

Also by Holly Rivers

Demelza & the Spectre Detectors
The Boy in the Post

1

'Free ice cream! Free ice cream!'

Kipling Brock burst into the Mailbox Menagerie, making Orinthia, Séafra and Taber jump. The three Shalloo siblings had been mucking out the animal enclosures all morning, and were now throwing fistfuls of mackerel to Geronimo and Gungho, the pelicans – their first bucketful of the day.

'Kipling, what are you talking about?' said Orinthia, looking up and pushing a strand of dark hair behind her ear.

Kipling, rosy-cheeked and button-nosed, threw

down his satchel and ran to his friends' side. 'There's a new ice cream van in the village!' he exclaimed breathlessly. 'And they're giving away free cones *today*!' He took a folded paper flyer from his pocket and opened it up. 'Look . . . !'

Orinthia wiped her fishy hands down the front of her overalls, before taking the paper and reading aloud.

TWO SCOOPS CREAMERY
INVITES YOU TO THE GALA OPENING
OF OUR NEW ICE CREAM VAN

Free cones for the first 100 customers

Sunday 1 August from 9 A.M.
Little Penhallow Village Green

'Sounds good, right?' enthused Kipling, standing over Orinthia as she read.

Orinthia nodded eagerly. At nearly fourteen, she knew that she probably shouldn't be feeling quite this excited about ice cream, but the first week of the summer holidays had already been a scorcher, and with the weather set to become increasingly warm this afternoon, a vanilla cone with a chocolate flake would *definitely* be a very welcome start to the day.

'What do you think, Tabs?' she asked, turning to her youngest brother. 'You fancy an ice cream?'

Taber didn't need to say a word – the way the scruffy-haired seven-year-old was jumping from foot to foot with a huge grin plastered across his face was answer enough. 'I'm going to bring Gungho!' he said, reaching into the pelican enclosure and scooping out the smallest of the two bucket-beaked birds. 'He can have a fly around over the green!'

'OK, but we need to leave now,' said Kipling, pointing urgently to the time on the flyer. 'We have to get there sharpish if we want to be one of the first hundred customers!' He flung the back of his hand to his forehead in his usual dramatic way. 'It would be an utter *tragedy* to miss out!'

Orinthia nodded, and was just unbuttoning her work overalls when Séafra cut in. At twelve years old he was nearly as tall as her now: lanky and growing by the day. 'Erm, I hate to spoil your plans,' he said. 'But there's still quite a lot of chores to finish here before we get ready for this afternoon's deliveries.' He nodded to the daily work rota pinned to the noticeboard on the far wall. 'The guinea pigs need brushing. The rats need their claws trimming before any more letters are ripped to shreds. And one of the porcupines' mailbags needs darning. We don't want to get in trouble with Grandy Brock.'

Orinthia tutted. She couldn't believe that despite everything they'd been through last summer, Séafra *still* insisted on being so sensible, so cautious. The sense of adventure he'd managed to muster while crossing the Atlantic Ocean in a freight crate hadn't lasted very long at all. And as much as she took her responsibilities at the Mailbox Menagerie very seriously, it was definitely OK to bend the rules occasionally (especially when free ice cream was concerned)!

'Relax, Séa,' she said, giving her brother a playful punch on the shoulder. 'Grandy Brock's busy doing paperwork in his office. We'll be there and back before he's even noticed we've gone. And I promise we'll get everything done before the animails go out on their first delivery.'

Séafra huffed in the way he always did when feeling under pressure. 'Fine. But we can't stay out too long.'

Kipling nodded and, cupping his hands around his mouth, wasted no time in shouting out to his siblings. 'Hey! You lot! Who wants free ice cream?'

His words rang through the verdant glass domes of the menagerie, echoing around the vivariums and fish tanks, aviaries and pens. Obviously intrigued by the sudden clamour, Petunia the octopus propelled herself

4

through the waters of her tank, before suckering herself to its glass frontage like a puckered orange star. Soon enough more of the animails looked up to see what was going on – raccoons scampered from their straw beds, monkeys swung through overhanging plants, and toucans swooped down from their perches. Even Zeno and Zelda, the Sphynx cats, took a moment to extend their long necks in observation, before returning to their saucers of milk.

'Did you just say what I thought you said?' shouted Peggy from up in the rafters. She was feeding chunks of ripe banana to Titus the fruit bat, who had just returned from his night shift and was now hanging upside down from his perch. 'Free ice cream?'

Kipling looked upwards. 'Yes! But only for the first hundred customers! We need to head to the village green NOW!'

Peggy nodded eagerly, and within a flash she'd hooked a leg around a nearby vine and was sliding down at breakneck speed. Titus the bat let out a loud *click-click* sound in protest. 'Sorry boy!' she shouted back as her feet hit the ground. 'But you're going to have to finish eating your breakfast alone today!'

By that point the rest of the Brock children, who had obviously overheard the exuberant commotion, had joined the huddle. Suki, the eldest of the brood, was half-drenched with water, having just given Bettina the pygmy hippo her monthly bath – always a soggy affair. Bramwell had a metre-long python hanging over his shoulders and was grappling with the tiny tree frog that was nesting amongst his tight black curls.

The smallest of the siblings, who had until recently gone by the nickname *Milky*, was now called Caspian – a moniker which Grandy Brock thought really suited the adventurous toddler (and one that would be much less a source of embarrassment for him in the future!). The toddler was naked apart from a cloth nappy secured with a large safety pin and came scooting forth on his bottom with a tiny white kitten on his lap. 'Ice cweeeam,' he garbled, wiggling his podgy fingers with glee. 'Me want ice cweeeeeam!'

'Yes, we're going to go and get some,' said Kipling, shooing away the kitten before hauling his little brother up on to his hip. 'Everyone else up for it?'

The rest of the Brocks nodded enthusiastically, wide-eyed. 'YEEEEES!'

'Well, what are we waiting for?' Kipling replied, looking as if he were about to explode with excitement. 'Let's go!'

In a flurry of enthusiasm, the children tugged off their wellington boots and unbuttoned their overalls, all the while chatting eagerly about what flavour cones they were going to order.

'I'm definitely going to have strawberry!' said Bramwell, licking his lips.

'Lemon sorbet for me,' said Suki.

'I wonder if they'll have knickerbocker glories?'

'With strawberry sauce!'

'And chopped nuts!'

'And hot chocolate fudge!'

Having made sure that all of the animal enclosures were securely shut, the gang made their way through the menagerie. But just as they were about to make their escape, the office door burst open. 'What's all of this caterwauling? Doesn't sound like there's much work being done in here.'

The children wheeled round to find Grandy Brock on the threshold, with Mr Malagasy, his ring-tailed lemur, perched atop his shoulder. Despite the heat the old man was wearing his usual three-piece suit, and had his favourite hunting hat pulled down over his head of rapidly whitening hair.

'We were . . . erm . . . just discussing what animals still needed feeding,' improvised Peggy.

'Well, that's funny,' said Grandy Brock, raising one of his bushy grey eyebrows. 'Because I'm sure I heard someone mention *knickerbocker glories*. And I don't recall any of my animals being fed on a diet of desserts!'

The children looked to the floor sheepishly.

'Well? Is someone going to tell me what's *really* going on?' pressed Grandy Brock.

Suki, caving under her father's glare, stepped forward. 'There's a new ice cream van in the village and they're giving away free cones today.'

'I see,' said Grandy Brock, crossing his arms. 'And you were going to abandon your duties to go and get one, I presume?'

'We weren't going to be long,' insisted Bramwell. 'We promise!'

'Please can we go, Grandy?' pleaded Peggy, clasping her hands together as if in prayer. 'Pleeeeease?'

The old man paused for a moment before smiling wryly. 'Of course you can! You'd be fools to miss out! But come straight back, OK?'

There was a huge cheer from the children, and having reached for their sun hats, they were out of the front door in a flash.

2

The sun was dazzling as the children crested St Sylvester's Mount ten minutes later, and they took a moment to catch their breaths as they looked down over Little Penhallow. Orinthia was so thankful to be out of her heavy work overalls, and was relishing the cool, cottony crispness of her summer dress, and the new open-toed sandals that Mum had bought her as an end-of-term treat. Nonetheless, an ice cream was definitely going to make the heat even more bearable!

Gungho, who had been circling overhead, suddenly came to rest on Taber's shoulder, cawing loudly with his white wings flapping erratically.

'Hey, what is it, boy?' Taber asked, trying to calm him.

The bird nodded towards the village green, and let out another loud squawk. Shielding their eyes from the sun, the children edged forward to see what he had spotted.

Their faces crumpled in an instant.

'Oh no, look at the queue!' said Bramwell, pointing to the ice cream van parked up on the village green. 'It's huge! We're *never* going to be one of the first hundred customers!'

Bramwell was right. Word of Two Scoops' gala opening had obviously spread fast and it seemed as though half of the village had turned up for a free cone. A long line of customers was already snaking its way from the van, around the duck pond, over the bandstand and down past the bowling lawn.

'Does that mean we don't get ice cream, Rinthi?' asked Taber, pulling at his sister's sleeve and looking up at her with disappointment.

'I'm afraid so, Tabs,' said Orinthia. 'Oh well, we'll just have to come back another day with our pocket money. Let's head back to work. And then I'm sure Mrs Gastaldini will be making something nice for lunch.'

'Yes, but spaghetti doesn't come with strawberry sauce and a chocolate flake, does it?' keened Kipling, running a hand through his hair in despair. 'This is awful! Ghastly! The worst day of my life!'

'Well, you'll just have to channel this raw emotion into your next recital of "To be or not to be",' joked Séafra. 'Come on, let's go. We're going to melt if we stay up here much longer . . .'

The children were just about to turn back the way they'd come when a young girl in pale-blue dungarees came bounding up the hill towards them. She was a bundle of energy, probably around eleven or twelve, with two blonde plaits and a little turned-up nose. 'Hey!' she called out, breathlessly. 'Wait up! Wait up!'

Orinthia felt her hackles rise. With everything that had happened with Mrs Pauncefoot and DI Snodgrass last year, she'd become rather wary of strangers. As much as she wanted to trust people, there was still a little voice inside that warned her to not assume that everyone was a friend. 'Erm . . . can we help you?' she replied tentatively.

'I just wanted to say hello,' said the girl, sweeping back her plaits as she came to a standstill. She looked up to Gungho and pointed. 'You're that lot with the post animals, aren't you?'

'Who's asking?' said Kipling curtly, obviously still in a mood, having not had his free ice cream.

'Kip, don't be so rude!' Suki huffed, giving him a nudge in the ribs. She turned to the girl and offered an apologetic smile. 'Sorry about him. He's just being a grumpy-pants because the queue for the ice cream van is so big.'

The girl looked back over the green and nodded knowingly. 'You came to get a free cone, huh?'

'We were hoping to,' said Suki glumly. 'But so many other people have turned up with the same idea. We're *never* going to be one of the first hundred customers.'

A mischievous grin spread across the girl's face. 'Oh really? Well, we'll see about that.'

Orinthia's nose crinkled. 'What do you mean?'

The girl crossed her arms. 'Well, it just so happens that *I* can get you right to the front of the queue.'

'Really?' said Kipling, suddenly revived. 'How?'

'Because it's *my* family's ice cream van!' the girl replied with a giggle. 'My mums own Two Scoops Creamery. We moved here from South Wales last week.'

The Brocks and the Shalloos all gasped with delight and Orinthia couldn't believe their luck. What a well-timed encounter!

'My name's Dotty, by the way,' said the girl, holding out a hand. 'Dotty Ambrose. Nice to meet you all.'

'You too,' said Orinthia, before introducing herself and the seven others.

'So are you all related?' Dotty asked.

Suki nodded. 'Peggy, Bramwell, Kipling, Caspian and I are brothers and sisters. And the other three . . . well . . . they're pretty much our siblings now too!'

On hearing what Suki had just said, Orinthia felt a warm glow in her chest. The Brocks definitely felt like family to her and she was so happy to hear that they felt the same. She looked to Suki and smiled, her heart full.

Kipling, whose mood had now turned a complete one-eighty, was eager to turn the conversation back to the ice cream. 'So you really think you can get us to the front of the queue?' he asked, jostling from foot to foot.

'Of course I can,' Dotty replied. 'I'm *meant* to be giving out flyers to passers-by, but we're hardly short on customers! Come on, I'll take you down to meet Penny.'

'Is that one of your mums?' asked Séafra.

Dotty giggled. 'No, Penny's our van! Short for the *Penny Lick*. Back in the olden days before cones were invented, vendors served scoops of ice cream in little glass cups, which everyone called penny licks.'

Kipling wrung his hands together in delight. 'Ooooh! They sound yummy!'

Dotty laughed. 'They were . . . until you caught cholera from eating out of one.'

The children looked at their new friend, mystified.

'The shape of the penny licks meant they were hard to clean,' Dotty clarified. 'So germs would get passed from one customer to the next.'

'*Urghhhh*, that's revolting!' exclaimed Bramwell. 'Vanilla with a side helping of disease!'

'Don't worry, you won't get ill from *our* ice cream,' said Dotty, before adding, 'Well, unless you eat it by the gallon!' She doubled over and mimicked being sick.

Orinthia chuckled. 'Sounds like you might be speaking from experience?'

'Erm . . . no comment!' Dotty replied. 'Now come on, let's go before my mums sell out!'

3

Dotty led the children down the hill, and as the *Penny Lick* slowly came into view there were shrill gasps of excitement. With its pale, mint-green paintwork and windows festooned with polka-dot bunting, it was a real beauty of an ice cream van. Its name had been hand-painted in gold across its side and the twinkling chimes of 'My Lady Greensleeves' came drifting from the brass horn on its roof. It had so much character, so much personality, and Orinthia couldn't help thinking that its headlights were a pair of twinkling eyes, and the painted grille between them, a smiling mouth.

As the children approached, Orinthia expected to be ushered right to the front of the queue, but instead, Dotty pulled them behind a nearby tree and brought her voice down to a whisper. 'OK, we'll just wait here for a minute,' she said, keeping her eye on the van.

'Hang on, I thought you said that we could go straight to the front?' said Kipling, looking slightly bemused.

'You can,' replied Dotty, crouching down into the shadows. 'But only when my mums' backs are turned. I don't want them catching you pushing in!'

She pointed to the van's large serving hatch, where two women in powder-pink aprons were busy fixing cones for the waiting customers. 'That's Pandora . . . or Mum,' she said, nodding to the taller of the two, who was svelte, with sun-kissed skin and a strong jaw.

'And the other one?' asked Orinthia, gesturing to the shorter, plumper lady, who had rosy cheeks and a dimple in her chin. Her blonde hair had been whipped up in a poofy bouffant mound, making her look a little bit like a knickerbocker glory herself!

'That's Pem. Otherwise known as Mam. She's Welsh, and has the same accent as me! Anyway, we'll wait here until they're distracted, then we'll make a run for it, OK?'

Understanding the plan, the Brocks and the Shalloos nodded approvingly – they were expert mischief makers themselves! As they waited for the right moment to make their move, Orinthia surveyed the *Penny Lick*'s large blackboard menu. Her eyes widened as she read what was on offer:

MENU

Vanilla

Mint choc chip

Strawberry

Butter Brickle

Chocolate

Top Banana

Raspberry Ripple

Tutti-Frutti

Orinthia felt her mouth watering as she re-read every flavour. They *all* sounded so delicious. How on earth was she going to choose just one?

A tug to her sleeve interrupted her thoughts. Dotty nodded to the serving hatch once more, where her mums now stood with their backs turned. Pandora was busy ringing up an order on the till, while Pem was reaching for a huge bottle of strawberry sauce.

'OK, let's go!' Dotty ordered, leaping to her feet and gesturing for the Brocks and Shalloos to do the same. They did, and like a band of undercover spies, they ran at a crouch to the very front of the queue, much to the dismay of the two pensioners who *should* have been next.

Pandora turned around to lean over the service hatch. 'Right, who's first?'

The pensioners opened their mouths to answer, when Dotty quickly jumped in, drowning out their grumbles. 'These children are, Mum. They've been waiting *ages*.'

On seeing her daughter popping up in front of her, Pandora blinked. 'Dotty, you're back. That was quick. Finished giving out all of the flyers already?'

'Erm . . . yes,' said Dotty sheepishly, pushing the remaining papers deep into her pocket. 'People were very eager to take them.'

Pandora nodded knowingly before looking down to the Brocks and the Shalloos. 'And who have we got here then, hmmm?'

'These are my new friends,' Dotty replied. 'They run the village post office. The one with all the animals!'

'Ah! The Mailbox Menagerie!' said Pandora with a wide smile. She turned to her wife. 'Did you hear that,

Pem? Dotty's new friends here work with the animal posties that deliver our mail!'

Pem turned. 'Well I never! How lovely!' she said, the gap between her two front teeth causing her to lisp slightly. 'Although I must say, when we first arrived in Little Penhallow I wasn't sure about having my mail delivered by animals and birds. But I've become quite fond of guessing which of your furry or feathery creatures is going to arrive on my doorstep every morning!'

Orinthia smiled. It was a sentiment she'd heard many times in recent months. When the Mailbox Menagerie had first opened, it had taken the villagers a little while to get used to buying stamps from red-bottomed baboons, or having their letters delivered by guinea pig or toucan or snake. But now, seeing a fruit bat pass overhead with a postcard in its mouth or an armadillo trundling along the high street pulling a mail cart was very much the norm.

'Anyway, have you decided what you want yet?' asked Pandora, nodding to the menu.

'Yes!' said Peggy, quick off the mark. 'There's only one flavour of ice cream worth having in my opinion and that's . . . chocolaaaaaate!' She rubbed her belly, letting her tongue loll from her mouth.

Pandora chuckled. 'OK, one choccy cone coming up. And I tell you what, because our mail is always delivered on time, I'm going to give you all *double* scoops!'

The children whooped with joy and Orinthia beamed at how brilliant the morning had turned out to be – ten minutes ago they'd feared that they weren't going to be able to sample any of Two Scoops' ice creams today, and now they were being given extra-large helpings!

One by one the children gave and received their orders. Séafra decided on the Butter Brickle which came sprinkled with chopped nuts. Taber, meanwhile, opted for Top Banana – a pale-yellow ice cream swirled with toffee sauce. Bramwell and Kipling both ordered strawberry, while Suki went for a tub of mint choc chip, which she'd share with Caspian.

'And what about you, my love?' Pandora asked Orinthia finally. 'Decided yet?'

Orinthia still hadn't made up her mind, and she let her gaze move from tub to tub, flavour to flavour, overwhelmed with choice. There were also an array of ice lollies on offer – strawberry splits, and cola rockets and apple coolers. 'I think I'll go for . . . Raspberry Ripple,' she said finally, pointing to the tub of milky-white ice cream marbled with deep-pink sauce.

'Good choice,' Pandora replied. 'It's actually *my* personal favourite. We only use the best seasonal raspberries and the thickest cream from the local farm. Farmer Newing's cows are the best milkers around!'

Orinthia's mouth began to water and she watched as the woman got to work, scooping up two more-than-generous boules and dolloping them atop a crisp latticed cone. 'There you go, lovely,' she said, handing it to Orinthia with a smile. 'An Ambrose *Super Bumper*! Lick it up quick before you get it down your jumper.'

'Thank you,' said Orinthia, receiving her bounty. 'It looks delicious.'

And indeed it was – sweet and creamy and cut with the tang of the fresh fruit. 'Dotty, this is the best Raspberry Ripple I've ever had!' she declared, turning to her new friend and licking up the river of pink cream that was running down her arm. 'What's it like having parents that sell ice cream for a living? Do you get to eat it every day?'

'Ha! I wish!' Dotty guffawed. 'Mum and Mam don't want me to end up like my *tadcu* – that's Welsh for grandad. He used to have a banana split for break-fast every morning and lost all of his teeth by the time he was sixty!' She curled her lips over her teeth, mimicking an OAP with a mouth full of gums. Everyone burst out laughing.

'I think they're quite hypocritical really,' Dotty continued. 'When Mam first met Mum she wooed her with knickerbocker glories and sundaes for a whole month! A year later and they had bought the *Penny Lick* together.'

'Will you be taking over the business when you're older?' asked Bramwell.

Dotty nodded. 'Definitely!'

'And as your friends, we'll be allowed free cones, I take it?' asked Peggy, cheekily.

Dotty smiled and brought her voice down to a whisper. 'Of course. Every day!'

'Is that so?' came a sudden voice from the serving hatch. 'Your mother and I might have to think twice about entrusting you with the business in future.'

Orinthia looked up to find Pem standing over them with an eyebrow raised.

'Erm . . . Mam . . .' said Dotty, trying to backtrack. 'I . . . I was just kidding.'

Pem ruffled her daughter's hair and laughed. 'Anyway, Dot, I forgot to mention but the local radio station are sending someone over in half an hour to do a live interview with me and Mum, so we'll be closing up shop as soon as we've given out all of the free cones. You'll be all right entertaining yourself here for a bit, won't you?'

Dotty nodded. 'Fine by me. I might go and feed the ducks.'

'Well, why don't you come back with us to Tupenny Mill?' suggested Orinthia. 'Grandy Brock won't mind. We can listen to your mums being interviewed on the radio, then we can show you around the menagerie.'

Dotty turned to her mother in a shot. 'Can I, Mam?'

'I don't see why not. As long as you behave yourself.'

'You're going to love it, Dotty,' enthused Orinthia. 'We have dogs and hedgehogs and monkeys and lizards and . . . well . . . you'll soon see for yourself!'

4

'So why did Grandy Brock start up the Mailbox Menagerie?' Dotty asked her new friends as they made their way back to Tupenny Mill. 'Didn't Little Penhallow have, well . . . you know . . . a normal post office?'

The Brocks and the Shalloos looked at each other and immediately burst out laughing.

'What?' asked Dotty, confused. 'What did I say?'

'No, no, it's nothing,' Suki replied. 'It's just that it's quite a . . . *remarkable* story, that's all.'

'I'm all ears!' Dotty replied, obviously eager to

hear the tale.

'Well, it all began when Grandy Brock got unfairly dismissed from his job at Royal Mail,' Kipling began. 'He'd been accused of stealing stamps, but was completely innocent of course.'

Suki nodded. 'He'd always loved animals, so he decided to set up a rival delivery service staffed by all the creatures he'd rescued and adopted.'

Orinthia cut in next. 'And that's when my brothers and I came along!'

As they continued their journey the children took it in turns to carry on the story. They told Dotty all about Mrs Pauncefoot's black market stamp dealings, and the Shalloos' summer jobs at the menagerie, and Geronimo's ill-fated maiden voyage overseas, and Taber's decision to post himself to New York to find her. With every development, every plot twist, Dotty's mouth fell open a little bit further, and her jaw was nearly touching the ground as she listened to Orinthia and Séafra's account of their transatlantic voyage in the *Penny Black*.

'So what happened next?' asked Dotty, eager to hear more. 'Once Mrs Pauncefoot and DI Snodgrass had been thrown in jail?'

'Well . . .' said Bramwell, coming to the final part

25

of their tale as they reached the front porch of Tupenny Mill, 'when everyone was home safe and sound, Grandy Brock got pardoned by the postmaster general, and the Mailbox Menagerie was officially opened.'

'THE END!' chorused everyone.

Dotty looked flabbergasted. 'Well . . . erm . . . wow,' she stuttered. 'I wasn't expecting all of that!'

'Neither were we,' said Orinthia. 'It definitely wasn't the summer holidays we'd been expecting. I've written all about it in my travel diaries if you want to have a read?'

'Oooh, just like that famous explorer, Ophelia Pearcart, used to do?' Dotty remarked.

On hearing the name of her hero, Orinthia gasped. 'You . . . you know about Ophelia Pearcart?'

Dotty nodded. 'Of course. Mam says that she's one of the most remarkable women to have ever lived. And apparently, my great-great-great-*tadcu* served her ice cream from his cart when she was passing through Wales on one of her expeditions.'

'Wooooow!' Orinthia replied, not quite able to believe what she was hearing. She and Dotty had so much in common! 'You *must* tell me more about it one day.'

Leaving their shoes in the porch, the children piled into Tupenny Mill, flinging their satchels and bags to one side. Orinthia never tired of stepping into the place's homely embrace. The yeasty smell of fresh bread still hung in the air from breakfast, and the sound of classical music was drifting peacefully from the little wireless radio.

Grandy Brock was snoozing in his armchair, an unfinished game of draughts splayed on the coffee table in front of him. Mrs Gastaldini – the Shalloos' cleaner and sometime babysitter – was asleep on the opposite settee, dressed in her usual floral tabard with a polka-dotted headscarf tied beneath her chin. She'd been spending more and more time at Tupenny Mill since being introduced to Grandy Brock the previous autumn. It had started with her coming over to do some ironing once a week, which quickly turned into her cooking dinner at the weekends. Then she'd begun helping with the gardening, and before long there wasn't a day that went by without a visit from the Italian woman. It was obvious to the children that she and Grandy Brock had grown very fond of each other, and they'd even caught them holding hands beneath the breakfast table one morning!

'Wakey-wakey you two!' said Peggy, marching

over and rousing the two grown-ups from their slumber. 'We've got a guest.'

'W-w-what?' spluttered Grandy Brock, jerking upwards. He quickly wiped away a string of drool hanging from the corner of his mouth and looked around. 'Oh my goodness . . . we must have dozed off. Serafina!'

'*Ufffa!*' groaned Mrs Gastaldini, rubbing her eyes. 'I was having a lovely dream about *pomodori* . . .'

'Only *you* could dream about tomatoes, Mrs Gastaldini!' said Séafra with a chuckle. 'Was there Parmesan cheese involved too?'

The other children laughed.

'You're a cheeky little thing, Séafra Shalloo,' Mrs Gastaldini replied, ruffling his black hair. 'But yes, come to think of it, *Parmigiano* did feature. And it was rather delicious as I recall.'

Grandy Brock heaved himself up from his armchair and let out a gravelly yawn. 'Anyway, did I hear you say that we have a guest, Peggy?'

'Yes, this is Dotty,' she replied, pulling their new friend forward. 'Her mums *own* Two Scoops Creamery and she got us right to the front of the queue!'

'Their ice cream is fantastic, Grandy,' enthused Suki. 'We got to have double scoops too.'

'Ha! I can see that,' said Grandy, looking to Caspian, asleep and sticky in Suki's arms. 'The little one's covered in the stuff, the mucky pup!' He took a cotton handkerchief from his cardigan pocket and wiped the toddler's mouth before turning to Mrs Gastaldini. 'If I'd have known you were coming over this morning I'd have got the children to pick up a cone for you too, Serafina.'

'Oh no!' Mrs Gastaldini exclaimed. 'I never eat ice cream outside of Italy! Nothing can compare to the flavours that my *famiglia* sell in their *gelateria* back in Naples!'

'Your family are ice cream sellers too?' asked Grandy Brock. 'I didn't know that.'

Mrs Gastaldini nodded. '*Si*, *si*. They make the finest stracciatella on the peninsula.' She threw her shoulders back with pride. 'Some things us Italians just do better.'

Grandy Brock and the children shared a knowing look. As much as they all adored Mrs Gastaldini, she did like to boast about the superiorities of her home country. The sun always shone brighter in Italy, the sea was bluer, the wine was smoother and the food was tastier. (Although she certainly didn't complain when presented with a traditional roast dinner of a

Sunday, and could wolf down a steak-and-kidney pie in two minutes flat!)

'Anyway, your mothers know that you're here, I take it?' Grandy Brock asked Dotty.

'Yes,' Dotty nodded. 'They're doing an interview for local radio at the moment so they said I could come here for a bit.'

Bramwell glanced at his wristwatch. 'In fact, they'll be live on air any minute. Let's listen in.' He dashed over to the radio and began to turn the dial, the speaker crackling as he skipped from station to station. Everyone gathered around, and as the radio arrived at the correct frequency, there was a burst of jingly music.

'*Good afternoon*,' came a low, honeyed voice. '*I'm Arthur Stallybrass, and I'm here in Little Penhallow with the village's newest business owners. Pem and Pandora Ambrose are the proprietors of Two Scoops Creamery, and this morning they opened their new ice cream van, the* Penny Lick, *by offering free cones to local residents . . .*'

On hearing Pem's and Pandora's names, the Brocks and the Shalloo children burst into applause, and an excited chorus of 'hoorays' and 'huzzahs' reverberated around the mill.

'This is so exciting!' said Suki to Dotty. 'Your mums are famous!'

'Oh, how I long for such stardom!' said Kipling wistfully. 'Such glory, such acclaim—'

Grandy Brock held up a hand. '*Shhh*, children. I want to listen.'

On the radio, Arthur Stallybrass continued with his interview. '*So how did the grand opening go this morning, ladies? You attracted quite a crowd by all accounts?*'

'*We couldn't have asked for a better reception,*' replied Pandora cheerfully. '*The people of Little Penhallow certainly like their ice cream!*'

'*And I hear that you're planning on competing in the inaugural Golden Udder Awards at the end of the month? Can you tell us a bit about that?*'

'*Well, it's a competition run by the International Dairy Guild which is being held in Bergen, Norway,*' Pem replied. '*Ice cream makers from all over the world will be entering with their best flavours. The winners will take home a trophy and a cash prize.*'

'*That's right,*' Pandora continued. '*So we need your listeners' help! As of tomorrow we're going to be asking the villagers of Little Penhallow to come forward with new flavour suggestions. At the end of the week we'll pick our favourite and it will become our entry for the competition. Just write your ideas on a slip of paper, and pop them into the ballot box at the* Penny Lick.'

'*Well that is exciting!*' remarked Arthur Stallybrass. '*But now it's time to head back to the studio for our live phone-in, where we'll be debating whether or not it's ever OK to overwater your rhododendrons . . .*'

Once the interview was over, Bramwell turned down the volume dial on the radio. 'Wow, those Golden Udder Awards sound exciting!' he said. 'Imagine being one of the judges. Tasting ice cream has to be the best job in the world.'

Dotty nodded fervently in agreement. 'Yes, I can't wait. But it's not *just* about how the ice cream tastes. Mum and Mam say the judges are expecting us competitors to put on a real show too. So we need to dream up an *extra*-special presentation to get their attention.'

Almost in unison, Peggy and Kipling jolted up, exclaiming, 'I've got an idea! I've got an idea!'

'Wow . . . that was quick,' said Dotty. 'I've been trying to come up with something good for weeks! I suggested that we dress up Mam as an ice lolly, but she wasn't keen.'

'My children have *very* active imaginations,' said

Grandy Brock. 'Never short of solutions!'

Peggy piped up first. 'I'm thinking that we should train up a couple of our animails to serve your ice cream to the judges. If they can deliver the post, then surely we can get them to deliver sundaes too. They could carry the cones in their mouths, or balance tubs on their heads!'

'I love it!' said Dotty with glee. 'Peggy, you're so clever.'

Everyone seemed to agree, apart from Kipling, whose face had dropped. '*Oh* . . . that wasn't exactly what I had in mind.'

'Oh don't tell me, you thought they could serve their ice cream while you read a soppy love poem or something?' Peggy jeered.

'No, of course not!' Kipling snapped. He bristled before murmuring sheepishly, 'I thought they could serve it while I was doing a tap dance, actually . . .'

Peggy rolled her eyes, and ignoring her brother's suggestion entirely, turned back to Dotty. 'So what do you all think? Shall we go with *my* idea?'

'It does sound spectacular,' Dotty replied before quickly adding, 'Not that I didn't like your idea Kipling, but—'

'It's fine,' Kipling retorted, swatting away the

comment as if it hadn't affected him at all. 'Not everyone has the sophistication to appreciate true art. But don't come running to me if animals and ice cream don't mix.' He crossed his arms with a huff, turning his back on the group.

'I was actually going to suggest that *you* choreograph some kind of routine for the chosen animails,' said Dotty. 'We can't have them just parading across the stage willy-nilly. It needs to look professional.'

Kipling spun round, his eyes suddenly sparkling. 'Really?'

Dotty nodded warmly.

Kipling was on his feet immediately. 'Yes, I could *definitely* do that! I can see it now – a snake serving strawberry sorbets while slithering a samba! Or cats doing the cancan while carrying caramel cones!' He proceeded to pivot across the room before taking Mrs Gastaldini by the hand and twirling her towards him. The old woman let out a squeal of delight, fanning herself with her hand.

'Well, that settles it,' said Peggy, looking very pleased with herself. 'Kipling will choreograph. But the next question is, which of our animails should we train up?'

'How about Helios, the new golden eagle?'

suggested Suki. 'We could teach him to zoom down on to the stage and dollop ice cream into the judges' bowls from above!'

'Nah, I think the porcupines would be better,' Bramwell countered. 'The cones would sit perfectly in between their spines. Nothing would be spilt and—'

'No, no, no,' said Séafra, shaking his head. 'Geronimo is the obvious choice. We could fill her bucket beak with the ice cream! It would look ever so impressive.'

'We'd have to clean her teeth first though,' said Orinthia. 'We don't want the ice cream tasting like mackerel.'

There was an explosion of excitement as the children pitched in with more and more ideas – shrieks of 'leaping lizards!' and 'dancing donkeys!' and 'waltzing wombats!' filled the air.

'Hang on a minute, what about *this* as an option,' said Grandy Brock, interrupting the cacophony. 'What if you trained up a couple of cows? They'd be much more in keeping with the nature of the competition. A *dairy* cow delivering *dairy* ice cream! What could be better than that?'

'That's a brilliant idea!' Dotty screeched.

'Genius!' Orinthia agreed.

'*Moooooo!*' Caspian brayed, much to everyone's amusement.

'But where are we going to get cows from?' asked Séafra. 'We don't have any in the menagerie.'

Dotty got up. 'From Farmer Newing's dairy farm of course! Mum and I go there every morning to get fresh cream to churn. I'm sure he wouldn't mind. Why don't we go ask him now?'

All at once the children leapt into action, scrambling to get their shoes.

'Woah, woah, woah!' said Grandy Brock, holding up his hands. 'You can't *all* go. We have our afternoon deliveries to prepare for, remember. Dotty, you can choose one person to take with you to the farm, but the rest need to stay here.'

'Gosh, OK,' said Dotty, obviously feeling a little put on the spot. She looked around, her eyes twitching with indecision, before her gaze stopped at Orinthia. 'Erm . . . Rinthi, would you like to come?'

Blocking out the jealous groans coming from the others, Orinthia nodded eagerly. She was delighted that Dotty had picked her and she couldn't think of a better way to spend the afternoon.

'But apart from Farmer Newing, I don't think we should tell anyone else in the village about what we're planning to do with the cows,' said Dotty.

'Why not?' asked Bramwell.

Dotty looked around surreptitiously, as if checking that no one was listening in. 'Because the Golden Udder Awards are a big deal. And the ice cream world is very close-knit. We don't want anyone hearing about our ideas and stealing them.'

'Oh come on, Dotty,' said Séafra. 'I know it's an important competition but you're making the whole thing sound like a spy novel!'

'It's true,' said Mrs Gastaldini. 'I know from experience how competitive ice cream makers can be. It's not all whipped cream and cherries, you know. My *famiglia* have to work very hard to stand out from the local competition back in Italy. I heard about a *gelataio* in Milan who once laced a rival's lemon sorbet with garlic!'

Dotty nodded and looked around the room, her face sombre. 'Exactly. So please, you must all promise to keep these plans a secret.'

5

Farmer Newing's dairy was just outside Little Penhallow, which meant another lovely long walk in the sunshine for Orinthia and Dotty. They zigzagged their way through the meadows on the outskirts of the village, kicking off their shoes and picking wildflowers as they went. There were blooms everywhere they turned – cow parsley, bluebells, corn-flowers, daisies – as if someone had scattered multi-coloured confetti across the landscape. There were apple trees too, their boughs heavy with pale-pink fruit.

Chatter came easy between the two girls and Orinthia loved getting to know her new friend a little better. She learnt that Dotty was twelve, her favourite colour was orange and that her favourite school subject was . . . lunchtime! She loved the smell of burnt toast, and could hold her breath underwater for more than a minute and a half. She was at her happiest when reading murder mysteries under her covers late at night, and had a growing collection of sea glass – over a thousand pieces. She reached into her dungaree pocket and pulled one out, holding it flat-palmed for Orinthia to see.

'It's beautiful,' said Orinthia, running a finger down the translucent turquoise surface of the stone. 'Where did you get it from?'

'Back home in Wales,' Dotty replied. 'We used to live by the beach. Every morning I used to go and see what the tide had brought in.'

Orinthia smiled. 'That sounds lovely. Why did you and your mums decide to move here to Little Penhallow?'

Dotty looked to the ground, catching her lip between her teeth. 'No real reason,' she said, kicking up a clod of dirt, not looking up. 'Our family were just a bit . . . different . . . to everyone else, that's all. We needed a change of scene.'

Orinthia didn't know for sure, but she thought that Dotty was probably talking about having two mothers, rather than a mum and a dad. She desperately wanted to tell her lovely new friend that there was nothing wrong with having a family that were *different*. She, Séafra and Taber only had their mum after all. And the Brock children had Grandy and a house full of animals and birds and insects! Was there even such thing as a *normal* family?

It was obvious that Dotty didn't want to elaborate any further though, so Orinthia said no more, instead putting a hand on her friend's shoulder, hoping that was enough to show that she cared.

Soon enough, the girls approached the large wooden gate which led into Farmer Newing's field. Beyond it, a rickety old scarecrow was rising up from amongst some bales of hay, its head made from a stuffed hessian sack with two buttons for eyes. A herd of cows had congregated around a nearby water trough, and they reminded Orinthia of the gaggle of old women that often milled around outside the green-grocers, moaning about the rising price of cauliflowers!

'Ah, young Dotty!' came a man's voice, as the girls swung their legs over the gate. 'Two visits in one day.

To what do I owe the pleasure?'

Orinthia looked up. A face was poking out from the cab of a gleaming red tractor: two dark eyes with weather-beaten skin, and a pockmarked potato of a nose. Orinthia hadn't met Farmer Newing before but she assumed that this must be him.

'Hello again!' Dotty replied, sweeping chaff from her dungarees as she strode towards the tractor.

The farmer jumped down and wiped his brow. He was a gangly man in dusty overalls, with a birds-nest of wild grey hair. If it weren't for the fact that he was moving, Orinthia might have mistaken him for a scarecrow too.

'What are you doin' here at this time of day?' he asked. 'Not needin' more cream already, are you?'

'No, no,' said Dotty. 'My friend Orinthia here and I have a proposition for you, actually.'

'Oh?' said the farmer, flashing a mouth of chipped teeth. 'And what's that then?'

'Well,' said Dotty, plucking up a long blade of grass and twiddling it between her fingers, 'I know this is a strange request, but we'd like to borrow a couple of your cows. It'll just be for a couple of weeks or so, then we'll bring them back.'

The old farmer looked befuddled. 'Eh? *Borrow* my

cows? What the heck are you talkin' about, girl?'

'Well, you know my mums and I are going to be competing at this year's Golden Udder Awards?' said Dotty.

'Pem and Pandora did mention it. Would be nice for you to bring home the trophy, eh? Not to mention that very generous cash prize!'

Dotty nodded. 'That's the plan. So we came up with the idea of training some cows to deliver our ice cream to the judges. We need to really impress them. We thought you might be able to help us.'

The farmer puffed out his cheeks, seemingly lost for words. He removed his hat and ran a hand through his head of wiry hair, before replacing it. 'Well, it's a nice idea, and I know better than anyone how clever animals are, but I don't think any of my cows would be capable of deliverin' ice cream, Dotty. I can barely get them to walk back to the barn of an evenin'—'

'But Orinthia is going to help me train them,' protested Dotty. 'She works up at the Mailbox Menagerie, and she and her friends are a whizz at teaching animals.'

'Ahhh, of course, I thought I recognized you,' said Farmer Newing to Orinthia. 'You're one of Amos's brood. It's a mighty fine service you're providin', I must say. Them animal posties are very reliable.'

'Thank you,' said Orinthia proudly.

'That's why I'm so confident we'll be able to train some of your cows,' Dotty persevered. 'What do you think?'

Farmer Newing let out a loud breath. 'Well, I guess there's no harm in tryin'. I can't loan you any of my milkers, but I *do* have a couple of cows that I've recently retired. They're not the most obedient pair though. A little stubborn to say the least.' He turned on his heel. 'Come on, follow me. I'll show them to you.'

He strode off in the direction of the farmyard, and Dotty and Orinthia turned to each other, grinning from ear to ear. Across the yard they went, picking their way through discarded bits of machinery, rusted oil drums and metal troughs. Young farmhands were calling out to each other, while a scruffy-looking mouser snoozed in the shadow of an old horsebox. Once they'd reached the large barn on the far side, Farmer Newing shooed away a flock of clucking chickens pecking at the large double doors, before going inside.

The barn was huge and had been split into differ-ent stalls, each strewn with sweet-smelling straw and housing a cow or two. There were sturdy-looking black ones spotted with white, smaller ones with soft brown hides, and even some of an almost reddish colour.

'So these are the two ladies I'd like you to meet,' said Farmer Newing, pulling open the gate to the furthest stall. 'Come quietly though, we don't want to spook 'em.'

The girls crept in, and found themselves face to face with two horned creatures with low-hanging udders the colour of pink blancmange. Their bodies were angular and muscly, and they each had a brass bell hanging around their neck.

'This one here is called Fosse,' said Farmer Newing, patting the flank of the closest cow. 'And that one over there is Falaise. They're both too old to be milked now, so I've been keeping them as . . . well . . . pets, I guess.' He brought his voice down to a whisper. 'Don't tell Mrs Newing, though – she's always on at me about the cost of keeping too much stock!'

The girls edged slowly towards the creatures. Fosse was the larger of the two, with a white hide spotted with patches of russet. Falaise was slightly smaller and fawn in colour, with a pale diamond-shaped patch in the middle of her forehead.

'Both are good-natured, and aren't skittish at all,' said Farmer Newing. 'But like I said before, they're not the best at following orders.' He reached into his pocket and brought out a small red apple. 'A little treat usually does the trick, though. Orinthia, as you're the most experienced with animals, why don't you give this to Fosse and see if she'll come to you.'

Orinthia took the apple and inched towards the larger cow. Her eyes were dark, framed by large, fan-shaped eyelashes. 'Hello girl,' she said, tentatively offering up the treat. 'You want an apple?' Fosse looked up and, after a few inquisitive sniffs, she opened her mouth and lapped up the piece of fruit with her long black tongue. It was as rough as sandpaper, and left Orinthia's fingers covered in slobber!

'There you go!' said Farmer Newing, as the cow scarfed the apple down. 'Seems as though she's more than happy to be friends.' He pulled out another apple and gave it to Dotty. 'Here, why don't you give it a try with Falaise?'

Dotty nodded, and repeated the exercise with the smaller cow. She too hoovered up the apple in seconds, and was soon nuzzling at Dotty's hand in the hope of another. 'So is it OK for us to take them back to the Mailbox Menagerie, Farmer Newing?' Dotty asked. 'They have more than enough space for them there and they'll be very well looked after.'

'Yes, yes, you're more than welcome. Amos and I have crossed paths a few times now down at the Drunken Duck and I know how much of an animal lover he is. I'm sure Fosse and Falaise will be very comfortable there for a couple of weeks.'

'And do you have any other handling tips for us?' asked Orinthia.

The farmer crossed his arms in thought. 'Well, the most important thing about cows is that they learn by association. So givin' them positive experiences will elicit positive behaviour . . . well, *most* of the time.'

'So basically we need to make their training sessions as enjoyable as possible, so they'll want to come back for more?' asked Dotty.

'Exactly!' said Farmer Newing. 'And take things slow. If a cow feels threatened or rushed it may react badly. If its tail's swishin' you're puttin' too much pressure on it, and you'll need to step back. Its happiness should *always* be your priority.'

Orinthia nodded earnestly as she took in the farmer's words. She enjoyed hearing him talk about his cows. He spoke about them with such respect and kindness and warmth – no wonder their cream tasted so good.

'Oh, and they both like listening to music on the radio if you have one,' added Farmer Newing. 'Jazz is their favourite, if you can bear listenin' to it that is!'

Orinthia laughed as she pictured Fosse and Falaise bobbing their heads to a bit of ragtime or bebop. What fun they were going to have teaching them new tricks.

'Right,' said Farmer Newing, clapping his hands together. 'I'll get the cows ready to leave then. I can't believe two of my old girls are going to be performin' on stage.' He reached for a couple of leather halters hanging from a hook on the wall, and began to prepare Fosse and Falaise for the journey back to Tupenny Mill. 'I tell you what, while I'm doing this, why don't you girls head into the farmhouse and ask Mrs Newing if she'll pour you a nice glass of milk? Fresh this morning, of course. She might have a couple of Eccles cakes too if you're lucky.'

Orinthia grinned. First ice cream and now cake. This was turning out to be a *very* good day indeed!

6

The two girls must have looked quite a sight as they led the newly acquired cows through Little Penhallow later that morning. Fosse had been more than a little reticent to leave the farm to begin with, and Falaise had tried a few times to wander back to Farmer Newing, but with a few apple-shaped bribes, they'd got going soon enough. As Orinthia and Dotty ushered them down the high street, children stared and pointed with glee, and many of the shop owners popped their heads out to wave hello as they passed.

Everyone but grumpy old Mr Parsons the

greengrocer, that was. 'Don't tell me you're going to be training *them* to deliver my post?' he called out as they went past. 'I've only just got used to the bats and the birds.' He was the only person in the village that still hadn't warmed to the idea of the Mailbox Menagerie, but in all fairness, that was probably because the animails were prone to pilfering things from his displays when his back was turned!

'Don't worry, Mr Parsons!' Orinthia reassured him. 'We're going to be training them to—' She stopped mid-sentence, remembering what Dotty had said about keeping their plans a secret. 'They're going to be pets, that's all!'

Mr Parsons nodded suspiciously. 'I hope so. I don't fancy waking up to cowpats on my doorstep every morning, thank you very much.'

Orinthia laughed nervously, thinking it best not to mention that Fosse had actually just stopped for a big poo only a few metres up the road. She quickly tugged at Falaise's reins to get the cow moving again, aware that *she* might do the same at any second.

At the end of the high street the girls crossed the village green, and before long they were nearing Tupenny Mill once more. They found Grandy Brock and the rest of the gang in a huddle out front, giving the daily briefing to the animails who were about to head out on afternoon deliveries. Bettina, the pygmy hippopotamus, was at their helm, with a large parcel strapped to her back.

'Bettina, you'll be delivering to the north-east side today,' said Grandy Brock, pointing out the route on the large map of the village which he'd spread across the grass. 'And you'll be assisted by Clara, Edith and Ediz.' He nodded to the three green lizards perched atop the garden table, each with little mailbags hanging across their chests.

'Edison and Albert, you'll be taking the streets surrounding the village green,' he called up to the two tangerine-billed toucans who were circling overhead clasping bundles of letters in their beaks. 'You'll have the rabbits and chinchillas helping with the—'

'*MOO . . . MOO . . . MOOOOO!*'

Grandy Brock's flow was suddenly interrupted by Fosse and Falaise who, having laid eyes on the brood of unusual animals in front of them, had began to low loudly. The old man turned sharply and his eyes immediately lit up. 'Hello you two! Or should that be you *four*?' he exclaimed, striding towards Dotty and Orinthia. 'Your mission was a success, I see!'

Even though they were all used to handling

animals that were far more exotic than the two cows, it didn't stop Séafra, Taber and the Brock children from running over to greet the new arrivals too.

'How magnificent!' said Grandy Brock, running a hand over Fosse's back. 'What a fine pair they are! Guernseys, am I correct?'

Orinthia nodded. 'The larger one is called Fosse and the smaller one is Falaise.'

'And Farmer Newing was OK with you borrowing them?' asked Suki.

'Yes, they're too old for milking now,' said Dotty, running a hand down Fosse's side. 'I think we've got a bit of a challenge on our hands, but Orinthia's confident we can train them.'

'Well, let's get them settled, shall we?' said Grandy Brock. 'I've already put down some fresh straw in one of the empty enclosures in the menagerie. We've got plenty of grain for them to eat, and Mrs Gastaldini is preparing some treats for them up at the mill. Orinthia, why don't you run in and tell her that they've arrived, hmm?'

Orinthia nodded, passing Fosse's reins to Dotty before running up the rickety steps to the mill. She pushed open the front door, almost tripping over Hadrian the hedgehog, who'd balled himself up on the mat. 'Mrs Gastaldini! We got the cows!' she called out.

There was no reply.

'Mrs Gastaldini?' she tried again, popping Hadrian on to one of the armchairs before meandering into the kitchen. A knife had been left on the chopping board, next to a tumble of half-cut pears. But the woman who had obviously been preparing them was nowhere to be seen.

'Hello?' Orinthia called out once more, checking first the bathroom before poking her head into the utility room. There was still no sign, and she was just about to head upstairs to check the bedrooms, when a sudden shout came from the direction of Grandy Brock's office. Orinthia turned on her heel and listened, and as the shouts continued, she realized that they were being spoken in Italian. Unless Mr Malagasy had picked up some words *in italiano*, it had to be Mrs Gastaldini!

As quietly as she could, Orinthia crept towards the office and, finding the door slightly ajar, she put her ear to the gap. She knew it was rude to sneak up on people, but she wanted to check that Mrs Gastaldini was OK. There seemed to be a lot of commotion – was someone in there with her?

'*Non mi puoi chiedere di farlo*,' came Mrs Gastaldini's raised voice from within. '*Non è giusto—*'

Orinthia couldn't understand what the old woman was saying, but it was obvious from her tone of voice that she was in the middle of an argument. When no response came, she could only assume that the old woman was speaking on the telephone.

With both curiosity and apprehension pushing her forward, Orinthia peered inside, making sure that she wasn't seen. Mrs Gastaldini was sitting at Grandy Brock's desk under the window, the telephone receiver clasped tight against her ear, her knuckles white.

'*Perché mi stai facendo questo?*' she yelled, throwing a hand into the air.

Startled, Orinthia leant back. It was strange to see the old woman so angry. Orinthia had known her since she was a little girl, and never in that time had she seen her so irate. What or who was causing her such distress? Should she wait around to find out? Maybe she should slink away and pretend that she'd not heard a thing . . . ?

But a loud gasp from within quickly caused Orinthia to peer through the gap in the door once more. Mrs Gastaldini was now on her feet, her face turning increasingly pale as she paced back and forth listening to whoever was on the other end of the telephone line. There was a long pause, before she let out a loud yelp. '*Non farmi scegliere, Nene*,' she protested. '*Non posso farlo—*'

She stopped mid-sentence. Whoever she was speaking to had obviously hung up. Mrs Gastaldini looked at the receiver before throwing it into its cradle, slumping back into the chair. Her eyes were glistening and she looked as if she'd just been given the worst news of her life.

Orinthia was in two minds about what to do next. Should she check that Mrs Gastaldini was OK, or give her some space? She knew that when *she* was in a bad mood, the last thing she wanted was people fussing. But as tears began to roll down the old woman's cheeks, Orinthia knew that she couldn't leave her alone.

'Erm . . . is everything all right, Mrs Gastaldini?' she asked, pushing the door open and edging into the room.

The Italian woman jumped, quickly wiping away her tears. '*Mamma mia*, Orinthia! You scared me!'

'I'm sorry. I didn't mean to,' Orinthia replied. 'I just wanted to check that you were OK?'

Mrs Gastaldini bristled and her tone suddenly sharpened. 'What were you doing loitering around outside anyway? Were you listening in to my conversation? It's very rude to spy on people, you know!'

'I-I wasn't spying, I promise,' stuttered Orinthia, slightly taken aback. 'I'll-I'll go. I'm sorry—'

'Orinthia, wait!' Mrs Gastaldini took a deep breath and composed herself. 'I'm sorry *bambina*, I didn't mean to shout. I was talking to my brother in Italy, that's all.'

'Everything OK? You sounded like you were arguing.'

Mrs Gastaldini looked back to the phone. 'My . . . erm . . . brother's been trying to convince me to move back home for some time now, that's all. He gets so upset when I refuse. Says that families shouldn't live so far apart.'

Orinthia nodded. That made perfect sense. She knew better than anyone that brothers could be tricky characters, that was for sure. She edged towards Mrs Gastaldini and put a hand on her shoulder. 'I bet your brother misses you, that's all,' she said warmly, before adding, 'and your cooking!'

'Yes, something like that,' Mrs Gastaldini replied meekly, staring into the distance before quickly changing the subject. 'Anyway, what was it that you came to tell me, Orinthia, hmm?'

Orinthia pushed her hair behind her ears. 'It's good news! Dotty and I managed to convince Farmer Newing to let us borrow two cows. Grandy Brock and the others are getting them settled in the menagerie. He said you'd prepared some treats for them?'

Mrs Gastaldini nodded, but was obviously still distracted. Her reaction wasn't the joyous excitement that Orinthia had anticipated. 'Please don't worry about your brother,' she said, trying to comfort the old woman. 'Séafra and I argue all the time. But we always make up in the end.'

Mrs Gastaldini nodded, but was obviously fighting back tears. Her shoulders began to heave, and she dropped her face into her hands, whimpering in Italian.

'Oh, don't cry, everything's going to be OK,' said Orinthia, taking a handkerchief from her pocket. 'I tell you what, why don't I finish cutting the fruit for the cows, while you freshen up?'

'No, no, I'm fine doing it myself,' sniffed Mrs Gastaldini. 'You head back to the menagerie and I'll come join you in a moment.'

'Well, if you're sure?'

The old woman nodded, and before Orinthia could say another word, she'd got up and fled the room. Almost immediately there was the loud *chop-chop* of the knife hitting the chopping board, and Orinthia thought it best not to probe any further.

7

Orinthia barely slept that night, buzzing at the thought of spending the next couple of weeks with Dotty and the cows. She awoke at dawn, eager to get back to the Mailbox Menagerie and start work on the new project. She knew that training the two cows wasn't going to be easy, but as Ophelia Pearcart had once said when describing her climb to the summit of Mount Kilimanjaro, '*Believe you can, and you're halfway there.*' In fact, Orinthia had popped into the local library on her way home from the menagerie the previous afternoon, and she'd managed to pick up a couple of books that she thought might come in handy. There was *How to Train Your Heifer* by a farmer named Toby Longman-Jones, and *The Encyclopaedia of British Farm Animals – Volume II* by veterinary surgeon L. Layzell. She'd even found a memoir entitled *My Udderly Brilliant Life* by Meg McClymont, whose cover depicted a curly-haired dairymaid drinking a glass of milk atop a Friesian cow.

Full of energy despite the early hour, Orinthia pulled on her work overalls, and with her library finds tucked inside her satchel, she skipped down to the kitchen.

'Wow, you *are* eager to start training, aren't you!' said Mum, who was sitting at the breakfast table, reading the *Little Penhallow Gazette* with her usual cup of black coffee. Orinthia and her brothers had told her all about Dotty, the cows and their plans for the Golden Udder Awards at dinner last night.

'We only have a couple of weeks before the competition,' Orinthia replied, pouring herself a glass of orange juice from the fridge before coming to join her mother. 'I don't want to let Dotty and her mums down.'

Mum smiled. 'In which case, I think you're going

to need one of my special breakfasts. Bacon and eggs do you?'

'Ohh, yes please!' Orinthia nodded eagerly. 'And *maybe* a couple of slices of fried bread too?'

Mum ruffled her hair affectionately. 'Cheeky thing.'

Orinthia sat back in the morning sunlight, watching as Mum gathered the ingredients she needed before heating some oil in the frying pan. Since the Shalloo siblings' adventure and eventual return from New York last year, their family home had been a much happier place. Mum had relinquished some of her duties at the family car dealership – Wheely Good Motors – to Uncle Max, which meant that she was now able to enjoy spending more time with her children. This time last year, Mum would have already left for the office, and Orinthia would probably have been pouring herself a bowl of boring old cornflakes. But now she was listening to the sound of eggs being cracked, and the sizzling of them hitting the pan. Life was much, much better.

'Where did you say the Golden Udder Awards were being held, love?' Mum asked, sawing away at a loaf of bread.

'Bergen in Norway.'

'Wow. Always fancied going to Scandinavia.

Dotty's not asked you to go with her?'

'I wish! It's Pandora and Pem who'll be presenting to the judges with Dotty on the day.'

'Well, I guess they're the experts,' Mum said, turning off the heat on the stove. 'Maybe I'll invite them all round for dinner one night? As long as they bring some ice cream for dessert!' She brought the frying pan over to the table and pushed the contents on to her daughter's plate with a spatula. 'There you go. That should set you up nicely for the day.'

And indeed it did. The breakfast was delicious and Orinthia ate with gusto, spearing up rashers of crispy bacon, and dipping fried bread into runny egg yolk. With belly full and with excited determination fizzing through her, she kissed Mum goodbye, and was out of the front door.

With the sun casting a gorgeous golden glow over St Sylvester's Mount, Orinthia arrived at the Mailbox Menagerie, and was delighted to see that Dotty's bicycle was already propped up against the front door. Dotty was obviously just as eager to get started as she was, and Orinthia couldn't wait to see her. Even though she got on perfectly well with Suki, Kipling and the rest of the Brocks, she felt she had a connection with Dotty that was really special.

'Morning, Dot!' she called out as she ducked beneath the low-hanging vines dangling in the threshold. As always she was greeted with the strong vegetative smell of plants and flowers, and the raucous cacophony of birds, mammals, reptiles and amphibians.

'Hello, Rinthi!' was the reply.

But it wasn't just Dotty who came meandering through the menagerie. Mrs Gastaldini was there too. Orinthia's thoughts immediately turned to the conversation she'd overhead the previous afternoon. She hoped the Italian woman was going to be in a better mood today – the way she'd flown off the handle and snapped had come as a bit of a surprise to say the least.

'Good morning, Mrs Gastaldini,' said Orinthia, nervously. 'What are you doing here so early?'

'Oh, I just thought I'd come and see if either of you wanted some breakfast before you got started with the cows,' replied the old woman. 'Dotty's already put in an order for marmalade toast. Would you like anything?'

'That's kind of you,' Orinthia replied. 'But I already ate at home, thanks.' She patted her tummy with satisfaction.

'Very well,' said Mrs Gastaldini. 'I've already fed Fosse and Falaise. What are your plans for them this morning, hmm?'

'Well I picked up these books from the library yesterday,' Orinthia replied, delving into her satchel. 'I thought Dotty and I could work our way through them to pick up some tips.'

'Oooh, good thinking,' said Dotty, taking the copy of *How to Train Your Heifer* from Orinthia's grasp and leafing through it. 'And *that's* why we're definitely going to reign victorious at the Golden Udder Awards this year!'

An odd look passed over Mrs Gastaldini's face that Orinthia couldn't quite read. 'Whether you win or not, it's the taking part that counts,' she said curtly.

'No, we're definitely going to win,' said Dotty, unflinching in her confidence. 'And that's a fact!'

Mrs Gastaldini headed for the menagerie door, and Orinthia was sure that she heard her muttering something to herself in Italian. It was obvious that she still wasn't quite herself after yesterday's argument with her brother. She was on edge somehow, and Orinthia hoped that she wasn't to blame for intruding.

As if answering her question, Mrs Gastaldini turned back sheepishly. 'I . . . erm . . . also wanted to apologize for how I behaved yesterday, Orinthia . . . in Amos's office. I was a little distressed.' Her bottom lip began to wobble and Orinthia could tell that she was once again fighting back tears.

Orinthia smiled, relieved. 'No need to apologize, Mrs Gastaldini. But I'm always here to talk if you want to.'

Mrs Gastaldini nodded then took a deep breath. 'Thank you, Orinthia. I appreciate that. Anyway, let me get that toast for you, Dotty.' She tottered off, leaving the girls to get started.

'Is she all right?' asked Dotty as they meandered over to the enclosure where Fosse and Falaise were bedded down. 'What happened in the office yesterday?'

'Oh, nothing really,' Orinthia replied, unlocking the gate to the sound of two loud *mooo*s. 'I just overheard Mrs Gastaldini in the middle of a rather heated telephone call. She was a little upset, that's all. Anyway, let's get these two out and about.'

It was obvious, however, that the cows were definitely less than eager to get to work. Fosse was far more interested in watching the other animals in the menagerie, and Falaise, entirely comfortable in her new straw bed, refused to even stand.

'Come on, girl,' said Orinthia, patting the flank of the smaller cow. 'Time to get up.'

The cow didn't budge, instead choosing to turn her head away with a disgruntled *mooo*.

'Falaise,' Orinthia repeated in her most authoritative voice. 'Up!'

Nothing.

Dotty, whose attentions were with Fosse, wasn't doing much better. Every time she managed to get Fosse's attention, the cow would quickly lose focus and revert her gaze back to one of the many reptile tanks or porcupine pens or one of the birds flying overhead.

'*Ufff*, this is hopeless!' said Orinthia, dropping Falaise's reins with a huff. 'How are we ever going to get them to deliver ice creams if we can't even get them out of the enclosure?'

'Maybe they're still hungry?' Dotty suggested.

Orinthia looked to the food trough which, despite having recently been replenished by Mrs Gastaldini, was already completely empty. She raised an eyebrow. 'I know cows have two stomachs, but surely they've had enough of a fill? We don't want to put them into a food coma before we've even started!'

Dotty stood for a moment, looking at the two cows

in thought. She obviously felt deflated, and Orinthia really hoped that her new friend wasn't going to give up on their plan.

But she needn't have worried. All of a sudden, Dotty punched the air, a huge smile spreading across her face. 'I've got an idea,' she exclaimed, jostling from foot to foot. 'Didn't Farmer Newing say that the cows liked jazz? Maybe we could play some music and see if they respond to that?'

Orinthia felt hope flood back through her. 'Yes, that's a great idea! Grandy Brock's got some old records and a gramophone back at the mill. Wait here. Let me go see if I can find something jazzy—'

'It's OK, I can go,' Dotty insisted. 'I can pick up my marmalade toast from Mrs Gastaldini while I'm there.'

Dotty headed off, returning ten minutes later with a brass-horned gramophone, and a few yellowing records clutched beneath her arm. 'Right,' she said, putting the gramophone down in the corner of the enclosure. 'I quickly realized that I didn't really know much about jazz music, so I just chose the records with the most interesting covers.'

'And your marmalade toast?' asked Orinthia.

Dotty shrugged. 'I couldn't find Mrs Gastaldini

anywhere. But Suki sneaked me a couple of cold sausages from the fridge, so I'm not complaining.'

The girls sat cross-legged on the straw-strewn floor of the enclosure and began riffling through the records. One, which had a picture of an old man holding a trumpet on the front, was entitled *Giles Mavis: The King of Brass*. Another, called *The Jazz Brothers of New Orleans*, depicted four men in black polo necks relaxing in a wine bar.

'This one looks quite good,' said Dotty, holding up *Masters of Bebop: Volume III*. 'Shall we give it a try?'

Orinthia, not knowing a single thing about jazz either, nodded, and having taken the record from its sleeve she placed it carefully down on the gramophone. She adjusted the needle and before long a piece of music came crackling through the brass horn, filling the room with a cacophonous riot of trumpets, pianos and drums.

The two girls immediately covered their ears with their hands.

'How can anyone listen to this stuff?' said Dotty, scrunching up her face in horror. 'It sounds like someone vomiting . . . backwards!'

Orinthia agreed. Could these jazz musicians even read music? Or were they just making up the hideous tune as they went along? It sounded awful!

The cows, however, thought otherwise. Within a minute they were on their feet, nodding their horned heads from side to side, and scuffing up straw with their hooves. Using a few chunks of apple as further incentives, Orinthia and Dotty finally managed to get Fosse and Falaise to follow them from one end of the enclosure to the other.

'The jazz seems to have worked,' said Dotty. 'But it's going to be a long couple of weeks if we have to listen to such a racket every day.'

Orinthia groaned. 'You can say that again.'

When Dotty and Orinthia returned to Tupenny Mill for lunch a few hours later, Séafra, Taber and the rest of the Brocks were already sitting around the kitchen table digging into the platter of sandwiches that Mrs Gastaldini had prepared for lunch.

'*Formaggio e pomodoro*, your favourite!' said Mrs Gastaldini to Orinthia, who promptly translated the sandwich filling as being cheese and tomato to a rather baffled Dotty.

'So, how are you getting on?' asked Suki in between mouthfuls.

'Good,' said Orinthia, taking a seat next to Kipling and urging Dotty to join her. 'Thanks to the *Masters of Bebop*!'

Grandy Brock, who was filling his plate at the head of the table, wrinkled his nose. 'Eh?'

Orinthia and Dotty looked to each other and giggled.

'The only thing that got them moving this morning were your old records!' said Orinthia. 'We borrowed a couple, I hope you don't mind?'

'Well I never!' Grandy replied with a chuckle. 'I used to love those tunes when I was a young man!' And with that, he began to scat just like the men on the record, *bee-bapping* and *ski-dooing* as he clicked his fingers to an imaginary beat.

'No! No more jazz!' said Orinthia, putting her hands to her ears dramatically. 'Please, no more!'

Grandy Brock laughed. 'Jazz is an acquired taste, that's for sure. But I'm glad you've found something to get the cows moving! *Ski-bee-bap-baaaap!*'

'You've not been working them too hard, though?' asked Mrs Gastaldini, placing a pot of tea covered by a woollen cosy down on the table. 'Remember what I said, it's not the winning that counts—'

'It's the taking part,' finished Orinthia, rolling her

eyes. 'Yes, we know.' That was the second time Mrs Gastaldini had said that to her and Dotty today, and it was beginning to annoy Orinthia a little. She knew that the old woman was feeling glum at the moment, but that didn't mean she had to dampen *their* enthusiasm.

The children chatted as they ate, talking about their animals and the ice cream flavours they were going to try next time they visited the *Penny Lick*. As soon as the sandwiches had been gobbled up, Grandy Brock brought out a large bowl of fruit salad. 'Children, before you dive in, Mrs Gastaldini and I have got something we'd like to share with you all.'

The Brocks and the Shalloos shared a few confused glances, wondering what was about to be revealed.

'Are you getting married?' asked Taber. 'Is there going to be a big party?'

Grandy Brock's face instantly reddened. 'No, no, nothing like that,' he spluttered, shifting his gaze to Mrs Gastaldini, who looked equally embarrassed. 'What I was *going* to say is that the cows aren't the only new animals joining us this week. Mrs Gastaldini has been so impressed with the work that we do at the menagerie that she's decided to have a go at training a creature of her own.'

'That's wonderful, Mrs Gastaldini!' said Suki. 'You're going to be brilliant at it.'

Mrs Gastaldini swatted the compliment away. 'Oh, I'm sure I won't be as successful as you, *bambina*. But I'm looking forward to giving it a go.'

'I think it's a great idea,' said Orinthia. 'And it might take your mind off everything that's going on with your brother too.'

Mrs Gastaldini blanched, and Orinthia knew immediately that she'd put her foot in it.

'What stuff with your brother?' asked Grandy Brock. 'Is everything OK, Serafina?'

Mrs Gastaldini bristled, and shot Orinthia an annoyed look. 'It's nothing, Amos,' she snapped, obviously uncomfortable with the topic of conversation. 'Just a little family disagreement, that's all. Nothing for you to worry about.'

'I'm sorry, Mrs Gastaldini,' Orinthia muttered. 'I didn't mean to bring it up—'

'It's fine, Orinthia,' Mrs Gastaldini cut in bluntly.

'I just—'

Mrs Gastaldini slammed her fork on to the table. 'I said it's fine!'

Orinthia gulped, not knowing what to say. Even though she felt guilty for what she'd accidentally divulged, she couldn't help wondering why Mrs Gastaldini was still being so secretive. She and Grandy Brock had become so close, and she was surprised at the old woman's refusal to open up to him about the pressure her brother was putting on her.

The atmosphere in the room had soured, and obviously eager to lighten the mood, Peggy turned to Mrs Gastaldini. 'So, what animal are you going to work with? You can help me with my snakes if you like?'

'Serafina has chosen to go for a feathered friend,' said Grandy Brock, and turning to the staircase, he put two fingers to his mouth and let out a shrill whistle.

There was a flash of grey as a large bird swooped down from the landing, slaloming through the spindles of the bannister before landing on the kitchen table with a squawk.

'An African grey parrot,' declared Grandy Brock. 'Her name is Zuni. Isn't she a beauty?'

She certainly was. Long-necked and svelte, Zuni had pewter-coloured plumage delicately edged with white. Her beady yellow eyes were set either side of a shiny black bill. Perhaps the most striking thing about her was her tail feather – pillar-box red in colour and as long and straight as an arrow.

'She's gorgeous,' said Séafra, running a finger down the bird's feathery chest. 'And parrots can talk, can't they?'

'They can indeed,' said Grandy Brock. 'They are vocal learners, meaning that they grasp sounds by hearing and imitating human voices. You teach a parrot to speak like you would teach a baby. That's why we thought Zuni would be such a great addition to the menagerie. Hopefully she'll be able to go out on deliveries and bid our customers a good morning.'

'Can she say any words yet?' asked Dotty, obviously excited to find herself in the company of yet another exotic creature.

Grandy Brock nodded. 'The previous owner had already started to train her. Listen to this.' He turned to the bird, and in a loud, clear voice said, 'Hello, Zuni. Hello.'

The bird dipped her head and with complete understanding, replied, '*Hallo, Hallo, Hallo.*'

The whole room gasped. The tone of Zuni's voice was shrill and croaky, but almost indistinguishable from a human's.

'That's incredible!' said Dotty in awe. 'What else can she say?'

'Well unfortunately she *has* picked up a few bad

habits which I'd urge you *not* to encourage,' Grandy Brock replied. 'But I'll show you just this once. I have to admit, it is rather funny.' He turned to the parrot again and said, 'Zuni, where's your bottom?'

The parrot immediately turned around and began to vigorously shake her tail feather. '*Bottom! Bottom!*' she screeched. '*Bottttttttom!*'

The children burst out laughing, which only encouraged the parrot. '*Bottom!*' she continued, shaking her rear end from side to side as she walked the length of the table. '*Bottom! Bottom!*'

'OK, Zuni, that's enough,' said Grandy Brock sternly, reaching for the bird and hoisting her on to his shoulder. 'The previous owner was obviously a bit of a miscreant.'

'Oh dear, let's hope Zuni doesn't start picking up any of Mrs Gastaldini's naughty Italian words!' said Bramwell.

'I sincerely hope not!' said Grandy Brock, turning to Mrs Gastaldini. 'You're not planning on corrupting your new feathered friend, are you, Serafina?'

But Mrs Gastaldini was staring into the distance, and seemingly oblivious to the parrot's antics. *Is she still thinking about her brother?* Orinthia wondered. If so, the feud was obviously really taking a toll on the poor woman. She started to wonder if there was a more serious family argument going on. Grown-ups were often very good at bottling things up.

Grandy Brock reached for the old woman's arm. 'Serafina?'

'Eh? What?' said Mrs Gastaldini, suddenly snapping from her trance. 'Sorry, Amos, I was miles away.'

Grandy Brock frowned, obviously concerned. 'Are you sure you're all right? You don't seem quite yourself—'

'I'm fine,' said Mrs Gastaldini, pulling her arm away a little too hastily. 'Now if you don't mind, I think I'll take Zuni up to the top of the mount. I need some fresh air.'

9

Orinthia was standing on stage at the Golden Udder Awards, a bright white spotlight beaming down on her as she looked out over a large audience. They were staring back at her with beady eyes, as if waiting for her to do something. Somewhere in the distance jazz music began to play and then out of nowhere, Fosse and Falaise appeared by her side. Orinthia looked around for Dotty, but her friend was nowhere to be seen. Frozen to the spot, Orinthia felt dread coursing through her.

'Well come on then!' shouted someone from the

audience. 'Get on with it!'

Panicked and not sure what to do, Orinthia began to pull at Falaise's reins, but the cow felt heavy, as if she were filled with lead. No matter how hard Orinthia tried, Falaise just wouldn't budge.

'This is rubbish!' bellowed someone else in the crowd. 'Get off! GET OFF!'

More heckles followed, and soon enough the jazz music had been drowned out by an onslaught of increasingly loud *boooooo*s. The sound rung in Orinthia's ears, and she looked around frantically, hoping that someone would come to her aid.

But instead, she was confronted by two squirming rattlesnakes that were hissing their way out of Falaise's eyes. Orinthia stumbled back as they opened their jaws, and with forked tongues quivering, they pounced—

'NO! GET AWAY FROM ME!' Orinthia sat up with a jolt, gasping for breath. Expecting the snakes to start biting at her flesh at any second, she held up her arms in defence, hoping she could escape their venomous teeth . . .

But the snakes had gone. And the booing had ceased.

When Orinthia finally plucked up the courage to

lower her arms, she found that she was in bed in her own room. The stage, the heckling, the snakes . . . they'd all just been an awful dream.

Orinthia ran a hand through her sweaty hair, breathing a huge sigh of relief. Why had she had such a horrible, horrible nightmare? She and Dotty had made incredible progress with Fosse and Falaise over the past week and there was no doubt in her mind that they were going to do brilliantly at the Golden Udder Awards. And besides, today was the day that they were going to be helping Pandora and Pem choose the winning flavour for the competition from the suggestions box. She had nothing to be worried about.

Even so, as Orinthia swung her legs out of bed and reached for her dressing gown, she couldn't help feel a horrible chill tightening her skin. The dream had felt so real.

Wiping the sleep from her eyes, she meandered downstairs and headed into the living room. She found Mum perched on the edge of the armchair, with the telephone to her ear and a rather worried look on her face. 'Yes, yes, Doctor Badeel,' she said. 'He feels ever so hot . . . and the spots are everywhere . . . he's completely covered.'

It was only when Orinthia found Taber lying on the sofa with a cold flannel pressed to his forehead that she realized Mum was talking about her youngest brother. His face and torso were covered in angry-looking red welts which he was scratching at incessantly.

She looked over to Mum, who quickly shooed her away from the sofa. 'Yes, Doctor Badeel,' she continued on the telephone. 'I'm sure I've got some calamine lotion here somewhere . . . and of course, I'll make sure he doesn't go near any other children . . . thanks so much for your help.'

Mum put the phone down and let out a long sigh.

'Mum, what is it?' Orinthia asked. 'What's wrong with Tabs?'

'Your little brother seems to have contracted chickenpox,' said Mum, coming to sit by the boy's side. 'That's why I was shooing you away. Dr Badeel says that it's highly contagious.'

Immediately Orinthia leapt to the safety of the doorway – there was no way she was catching chickenpox a week before the Golden Udder Awards; she didn't have time to be ill!

'Mummy, I'm so itchy,' Taber groaned.

'I know, poppet,' Mum replied softly. 'I'll go and

get some special ointment from the medicine cabinet to put on your spots. That should calm them down a little.'

'And then I can go to the *Penny Lick* with Rinthi and Séafra?'

'I'm afraid not, little man,' Mum replied with a frown. 'You can't leave the house until you're better, I'm afraid. Doctor's orders.'

The little boy's face crumpled. 'But I'm going to miss out on picking the ice cream flavour for the competition. It's not fair.'

'I know, my darling. Maybe your sister can bring you back an ice lolly to help keep your temperature down? Although saying that, I better check *your* temperature before you go out, Rinthi. We don't want to be passing this nasty lurgy all around the village, do we?'

She reached for the thermometer on the coffee table, and shook it out before popping it under her daughter's tongue. The minute-long wait for the result was agonizing, and Orinthia hoped more than anything that she didn't have a high temperature. For a horrible moment she thought that maybe the nightmare last night had actually been a fever dream – that chickenpox had caused her to hallucinate. She had woken up sweating after all . . .

But when Mum pulled out the thermometer Orinthia was relieved to find that her temperature was normal.

'Thirty-seven degrees,' said Mum. 'But if you feel like you're getting even a hint of a fever, Rinthi, I want you to come straight home, OK?'

Orinthia nodded, and as soon as Séafra had been given the all-clear too, the siblings headed down to the village green, both praying that no red spots would appear on their faces before they reached the *Penny Lick!*

'Ah! Just in time!' said Dotty, emptying out the ballot box with her mums as Orinthia and Séafra arrived at the ice cream van. Grandy Brock and his children were already there, leisurely reclining on the village green and enjoying the early morning breeze. Mrs Gastaldini was nowhere to be seen, however, and Orinthia could only assume that she still wasn't in the best of moods. She'd been more and more grouchy all week – her usual smile had been replaced with a worried frown, her once-sparkling eyes were dulled and distant. Orinthia had half-wondered about contacting the old woman's brother herself to make him aware of the effects of their feud, but had thought better of it – she didn't want to offend Mrs Gastaldini any further.

'So have we got lots of suggestions?' asked Séafra.

'Oh yes! People have been so eager to give us their flavour ideas,' said Pandora. 'It's going to be a tough job choosing a winner, that's for sure.' She began riffling through the idea slips that the villagers had left. 'Mr Barnabas has suggested *bubblegum* . . . The ladies of the Women's Institute have gone for *maple and walnut* . . . and listen to this one . . . *baked beans on toast*!'

The children grimaced.

'Who suggested *that*?' asked Séafra.

Pandora looked to Grandy Brock knowingly.

'Guilty!' he replied with a mischievous chuckle. 'Just a little joke.'

'I think baked bean ice cream could be quite tasty,' said Kipling with a shrug.

'Weirdo,' Peggy replied, shaking her head. 'Unless it was with chocolate sauce, of course!'

Kipling tutted. 'And you say *I'm* the weirdo!'

Pem clapped her hands together. 'Right, let's get started. Put any that you think are good in a "yes" pile, and discard any others.' She handed everyone a wedge of slips to look through.

'But nothing *too* odd!' added Pandora, looking to Grandy Brock with a raised eyebrow. 'Let's hope *someone* hasn't submitted any more joke flavours.'

Orinthia was quick off the mark to start putting suggestions in her 'yes' pile. She loved the sound of black cherry, spicy ginger snap, Nutty Nut and chocolate éclair. She wasn't entirely sure about the cucumber sorbet which Ms Cardinal, her teacher, had suggested, and Farmer Newing's Stinky Blue Cheese was a definite 'no'!

'Oooh, this is a good one,' said Séafra, holding up a slip with the words 'home-made lemonade' scrawled across it.

'That should definitely be a *yes*,' Dotty agreed. 'Sounds so refreshing. We could top it with sherbet to make it really fizz!'

Séafra nodded, almost drooling.

The search continued with glee, the children's 'yes' piles growing taller and taller by the minute. But narrowing down the suggestions was tricky. For the next hour ideas went back and forth, and cases were made for different flavours. Kipling made an extremely dramatic speech in favour of the equally dramatic sounding Rhapsody in Blackcurrant, while Bramwell was adamant that buttery popcorn sounded the best.

Pem, who'd so far discarded most of the idea slips she'd read, suddenly yelped out in excitement. 'Hang on, hang on! I think I might have found the best suggestion so far. What do you all think about jam roly-poly pudding? It used to be one of my favourite desserts as a child.'

'What's jam roly-poly?' Bramwell asked.

'Ooooh, it's absolutely delicious!' Pem replied, licking her lips. 'A steamed suet pudding rolled up with jam and served with plenty of custard.'

'And it's something that's unique to the British Isles,' said Pandora enthusiastically. 'Something that competitors from other countries would never come up with.'

'That settles it!' said Dotty with a nod. 'We better get to work on the recipe. Who fancies coming down to the creamery to help me and Mam?'

'ME!' came a chorus of replies from the Shalloos and the Brocks.

'Is that OK, Amos?' Pem asked Grandy Brock. 'We won't be taking your children away from their duties at the menagerie?'

'No, no, that's fine,' Grandy Brock replied with a wink. 'I'm sure I'll be able to manage without them for once. Serafina can help me anyway.'

Excited at the prospect of spending the afternoon making ice cream, the children made to move, when something suddenly caught Pandora's eye. 'Hang on, I think we might have missed one of the suggestions,' she said, fishing around in the bottom of the ballot box. Taking out the final paper slip, she began to read.

A sudden gasp slipped from between her lips.

'What is it, Mum?' Dotty asked. 'Another good one?'

'It's . . . it's nothing,' backtracked Pandora, trying to hide the slip of paper. 'Just a silly suggestion, that's all.'

But the woman's face was as white as a sheet, and her hands were trembling.

'Come on, Mum, show us what it says,' said Dotty. She snatched the slip from her mother's grasp and began to read the handwritten note aloud to the rest of the group:

This is a warning.
Do not, under any circumstances,
enter the Golden Udder Awards.
Pull out of the competition immediately.
If you ignore this demand,
there will be serious consequences
for you and your family.

'That's . . . that's horrible!' said Orinthia, not quite believing what she'd just heard. 'Who would write something like that? It's not another one of your practical jokes, is it, Grandy Brock?'

'What? No!' he blurted out. And it was clear from the old man's incredulous stare that he was telling the truth.

'I bet it was grumpy Mr Parsons, the greengrocer,' said Kipling, jumping to conclusions immediately. 'He's always moaning about things. And Orinthia, didn't you say that he'd been complaining about the music coming from the *Penny Lick* the other day?'

Orinthia nodded. It was true of course, but surely not even Mr Parsons would go to such vengeful measures?

'It's obviously just a silly prank,' said Pandora with a meek laugh, trying to brush off the children's concerns. 'A wind-up, that's all.' She looked to her wife as if to say, *Isn't that right?*

'Exactly,' said Pem. 'Nothing to worry about . . .'

But there was a nervous wobble in the Welsh woman's voice and a look on her face that made it quite obvious that she didn't believe the words coming out of her mouth. Grandy Brock's expression was identical, and Orinthia felt her skin tighten with prickles.

'Mum, I'm scared,' said Dotty, her usual upbeat demeanour now one of terror.

'Me too,' said Séafra. 'I don't want anything bad to happen to you all. Maybe you *should* pull out of the competition.'

'Absolutely not!' Pandora replied, snatching back the slip of paper and stuffing it into her apron pocket. 'As I said, this is just a silly prank and we shan't be bullied into anything!' She clapped her hands together as if it were the end of the matter, but not before glancing once more in her wife's direction. 'Now, I want you all to go along to the creamery with Pem and work on the recipe for the new flavour like we said. And promise me that you won't give this silly note another thought, OK?'

Dotty nodded reluctantly, and gave her mum a big squeeze. 'OK.'

'Good. Now off you go. I want you to come home with the best jam roly-poly ice cream you can make!'

The children headed off across the village green, but still shocked by what had just happened, Orinthia couldn't help but take a final backwards glance at the *Penny Lick*. It was then that she realized that instead of following them, Pem had in fact hung back to talk to Pandora and Grandy Brock.

'Come on, Rinthi, hurry up!' shouted Suki from up ahead.

'I'll catch up with you!' Orinthia called back, pretending to tie her shoelace in order to watch what was going on. 'I won't be long.'

The three grown-ups were deep in serious conversation, their faces forlorn and their postures rigid. They were obviously having one of those 'private talks' that adults liked to have when something wasn't right. Orinthia watched intently as Pandora took the note from her pocket to examine it once more. Grandy Brock shook his head, putting a hand on her shoulder in comfort. Even though the three grown-ups had dismissed the note in front of the children, it was very obvious from their behaviour that they saw it as a real threat.

10

Even though it was still very much on Orinthia's mind, by the time they'd reached Two Scoops Creamery the other children seemed to have forgotten about the horrible threat the Ambroses had just received. Dotty and Pem's chatter had quickly turned to what ingredients would be needed to replicate the flavours of a jam roly-poly pudding, and seeing the smile back on her friend's face, Orinthia thought it best not to tell Dotty about the secret conversation she'd just witnessed between her mums and Grandy Brock.

'OK, here we are,' said Pem, holding out her arms as she led them up to the creamery. It was nestled under an arch of the railway bridge, which she said once upon a time had been used for storing sleepers, ballast and track. A mint-green sign, the same colour as the *Penny Lick*, hung over the double doors in welcome, with the words 'Two Scoops Creamery' emblazoned across it in a loopy, pale-pink font. 'You're going to need to put these on before we go in,' Pem continued, leading the children into a small entrance room before handing each of them a white hair net. 'We take hygiene very seriously.'

'Ha! You look like a bag of oranges, Kip!' Peggy jeered as Kipling pulled his net over his marmalade-coloured mop.

'Well *you* look like a trout that's just been hauled out of the sea!' the boy retorted, 'but if I were a fisher-man I'd throw you straight back overboard!'

'You all look as silly as each other,' Pem reassured, tucking her blonde curls into her own hair net. 'But we can't have any loose hairs getting into the ice cream.'

Beyond the entrance hall was another set of double doors. As Dotty pushed them open, the first thing that hit Orinthia was the incredible aromas coming from within. All the yummiest smells in the world seemed to waft towards her all at once, engulfing her like a blanket. She breathed in deeply, enjoying the moment – she detected toffee, cocoa, roasted nuts, vanilla, candied fruits, brown sugar, marshmallow and her favourite of them all – cinnamon.

'Welcome to the Ideas Room!' said Dotty with a smile. 'This is where the magic happens!'

Once the doors were closed behind them, all the children could do was stand and stare. They were in a sprawling, cavernous space with brick walls and a low, curved roof. All around there were contraptions and machines, appliances and mechanisms, each one playing its part in the ice cream-making process. Pipes ran all over the ceilings and walls, dials whirred, lights blinked, levers spun and gears turned.

Orinthia looked around curiously, trying to take it all in. There were gadgets that peeled and chopped nuts, and gizmos that stirred and thickened cream. To her left she spotted a contraption cracking eggs by the dozen, and to her right a huge mangle was squeezing juice from strawberries and raspberries. Copper-bottomed saucepans were bubbling away on a large stove, the smell rising from them sweet and deep and honeyed. *Caramel perhaps?* Orinthia thought. *Or golden syrup?*

The most impressive sight of all was the ingredients shelves that spanned the entirety of the furthest wall. Orinthia's gaze jumped between jars of chocolate chips and vanilla pods, sugar sprinkles and chunks of honeycomb. There were bottles of jewel-coloured syrups and tall phials of fruit cordials.

'Dotty, Pem, this is amazing!' she said, looking around in awe. 'What a set-up you have.'

'A girl from the village called Demelza Clock helped Mum and Mam design all of the machines,' Dotty replied. 'She's a brilliant inventor – a real whizz with soldering irons and screwdrivers!'

'Ha! Maybe I should hire this Demelza girl to invent some contraptions for the Mailbox Menagerie,' said Suki. 'A claw-clipping machine would definitely come in handy!'

'Not to mention an automated pooper scooper!' added Kipling.

Pem clapped her hands together before reaching for a large wooden spoon. 'Right, let's get started on this jam roly-poly recipe,' she declared. 'I've got some plain vanilla ice cream already churned, so why don't you go and find the other ingredients? We'll need flour, butter and suet for the pudding mix and there's plenty of Mum's home-made strawberry preserve in the pantry.'

Throughout the afternoon Pem tweaked and re-tweaked the recipe several times, appearing on the hour with new variations of the ice cream for the children to try. After their first round of licking and slurping, everyone agreed that the inaugural batch wasn't quite sweet enough, and would definitely benefit from more ripples of the yummy strawberry jam.

The second batch was delicious but the children all thought that it could do with being creamier.

The third batch was very nearly there, just needing a few more chunks of the roly-poly sponge to add texture.

'OK, this is definitely spot on!' said Pem, bringing out the fourth batch as the afternoon drew to an end. It was the colour of a perfectly steamed suet pudding, topped with a glistening, jammy sauce. Without needing any more encouragement, eight spoons were eagerly plunged into the tub.

For a moment there was complete silence.

'Well?' asked Pem, clenching her fists with anticipation.

The Brocks and the Shalloos looked at each other,

and without needing to confer, burst into rapturous applause.

'It's *sooo* yummy!' exclaimed Dotty, patting her mother on the back.

'Perfection!' Séafra agreed.

Caspian didn't even need to utter a word to express his appreciation – the toddler had plunged his face into the tub and was licking away with wanton abandon!

'That's settled then!' said Pem, dabbing her brow with a handkerchief and looking very satisfied. 'I'll get the final recipe written down, ready to—'

Pem flinched mid-sentence, distracted by a sudden scritching, scratching, scrabbling sound coming from the other side of the Idea Room's door. It was as if someone was trying to get in, and Orinthia could tell from Pem's quickly widening eyes that her thoughts had immediately turned to the threatening note.

'Hello?' Pem called out. 'Who's there?'

The rattling continued.

'Hello?'

No answer.

Brandishing her wooden spoon, Pem turned to the children. 'Stay here,' she whispered, her face ashen. 'Don't move.'

She edged towards the door with caution, and with a trembling hand prised it open just the tiniest bit.

She immediately recoiled with a yelp, shielding her face with her hands. A grey and red bird had swooped inside, flapping its wings ferociously and squawking at the top of its lungs.

It was Zuni!

'Oh my goodness me!' gasped Pem, ducking quickly as the parrot zoomed over her head. 'I thought it might have been . . . well . . .'

She didn't finish her sentence, but Orinthia knew what she had been thinking – that whoever had written the threatening note had been trying to break into the creamery.

No one else seemed to have noticed though, and they were too busy fussing over the parrot's unexpected entrance.

'Hey girl, what are you doing in here?' said Dotty, holding out a welcome hand. Zuni swooped towards her, but no sooner had the parrot landed on the back of her palm, than she began to peck at Dotty's fingers.

'*Ouch!*' Dotty yelped, pulling back her hand in pain as the bird let out a loud screech. 'She bit me! *Ouuuuuch!*'

'Oh my goodness, Dotty! Are you OK?' Suki

exclaimed, quickly coming to the girl's side and shooing the parrot away with a loud clap. 'We must have startled Zuni and she got scared.'

Dotty looked down at her thumb, which was dripping with blood. 'I'm . . . I'm fine,' she said, shaking it out. 'It's only a scratch.'

'It looks like more than a scratch to me!' exclaimed Pem, running to her daughter's aid. She took her handkerchief from her pocket and pulled it tightly around the wound. 'Come on, we need to get this cleaned up and bandaged at once. And we're going to need to get rid of all the ice cream we made this afternoon – that parrot might have contaminated it and we can't take such a risk!'

She quickly led Dotty out of the Ideas Room, leaving the other children staring up at Zuni, agog. The grey parrot was now nestling up in the rafters of the curved roof, her head hung and her feathers ruffled.

'Well it looks like Mrs Gastaldini needs to do a *lot* more training with her,' said Kipling with a frown.

'She just got spooked, that's all,' said Suki. 'Probably flew in here and felt trapped.' She reached for a chair to stand on. 'Come on, let's try and lure her down.'

'I'll leave that with you,' said Kipling with a splutter. 'I'd like to go home with all of my fingers intact, thank you very much!'

11

Back at Tupenny Mill, Grandy Brock and Mrs Gastaldini were in the kitchen preparing supper. There was already a huge bowl of spaghetti bolognese in the middle of the table, as well as a crisp green salad and a chunk of Parmesan cheese waiting to be grated.

'Mrs Gastaldini, you'll never guess what,' said Suki, kicking off her shoes before retrieving Zuni from inside her satchel. (The parrot had been put in there for safekeeping once the children had finally managed to lure her down from the rafters, in the hope that it would calm her down.) 'Zuni somehow followed us down to Two Scoops!'

Mrs Gastaldini looked up from the table with a gasp. 'Oh Zuni! *Uccellino mio!* What have you being doing, hmm?'

The parrot flew across the room, coming to roost on the old woman's lap. Mrs Gastaldini looked down at the bird scornfully. 'Now don't you ever go flying off again, do you hear me? That was very dangerous!'

'You can say that again,' said Kipling. 'She got scared and bit Dotty. Pem had to bandage up her finger!'

The Italian woman stiffened suddenly, her brow darkening. 'What? But that can't be possible! Zuni would never do such a thing.'

'I'm afraid it's true, Mrs Gastaldini,' said Bramwell. 'But I'm sure it was just an accident. She was just spooked by being handled by someone new, I think. Nothing that a bit more training won't sort out.'

'Excuse me? Are you accusing me of doing a bad job with her, Bramwell?'

Bramwell, completely taken aback, began to splutter. 'W-w-what? No, of course not. I—'

'Well it sounded as though you were!' Mrs Gastaldini harrumphed.

Orinthia's nose crinkled with confusion. This was at least the third time that Mrs Gastaldini had been snappy with one of them recently. Orinthia was starting to wonder if it wasn't just the stuff with her brother that was on her mind. Was there something else that was putting her in such a cross mood?

'I think it was all just a bit of a misunderstanding, Serafina,' said Grandy Brock, trying to mediate, but obviously just as perplexed as everyone else. 'The sproglets think you're doing a fantastic job with Zuni, isn't that right everyone?'

The children nodded sheepishly, not daring to exacerbate the situation.

Mrs Gastaldini looked to the floor, and Grandy Brock reached out a comforting hand. 'You see?'

'Thank you, Amos,' said Mrs Gastaldini, squeezing his arm affectionately and causing his cheeks to immediately flush. She paused for a moment. 'I'm sorry everyone. I know I've been a little . . . *iraconda* . . . grumpy, over the past week. The truth is, my brother in Italy has been on at me to go back to Napoli for a while now, and' – she paused, taking a deep breath – 'I recently found out it's because he's not very well. I'll be returning to Italy next week. I've wanted to tell you all, but I didn't know how.'

The news came as a huge shock to everyone, including Grandy Brock. 'Oh Serafina, I'm so sorry to hear that,' he said. 'Will your brother be OK?'

'I do hope so, but he's going to have to go to the *ospedale* . . . hospital . . . for a little while.'

'Does he have chickenpox like Taber?' Peggy asked.

'No. It's a little more serious than that. And that's why I must go home. He needs me by his side. My *famiglia* need me.'

Grandy Brock nodded, but was obviously devastated. 'And how long will you be gone for?'

'The truth is, I don't know, Amos.'

Orinthia didn't know what to say. Poor Mrs Gastaldini. How awful it must have been for her keeping such horrible news to herself.

'I love you all,' said Mrs Gastaldini, her eyes glistening. 'You have welcomed me into your home, and I'm going to miss you so so much.'

Orinthia went to her side and rested her head on her shoulder. She smelt of cooking and laundry powder and her beloved *pomodori*. She was going to miss her terribly too.

12

'Dotty! Rinthi!' Kipling shouted down from the landing. 'Are you ready to go and start work on the dance steps?'

With only a week to go until the competition, and with Fosse and Falaise now understanding the commands to *WALK*, *WAIT*, *LIE DOWN*, *REVERSE* and *BOW*, it was time for Kipling to start teaching the cows his choreography. He'd been working on a routine ever since Dotty had set him the challenge, but he'd kept his progress very much under wraps. Each night after finishing at the menagerie he'd been retiring to his room, putting the music of *The Jazz Brothers of New Orleans* on loop, and leaping and twirling around until the early hours. Every time Orinthia and Dotty had tried to get a glimpse of the moves he was working on, he'd shooed them away, locking his door firmly behind him and insisting that *great choreographers never reveal the inner workings of their process!*

Orinthia looked up and as Kipling came prancing down the stairs, she saw that he was wearing a pale-pink tutu over his trousers, complete with a fluffy wrap-around cardigan and a pair of satin ballet shoes. He had his basket of ribbons and silks under his arm and was grinning from ear to ear.

She couldn't help but beam at the sight. She loved how her friend was completely unapologetic about what made him happy. Not many boys in the village would be brave enough to wear a dance skirt, even if they wanted to, but Kipling didn't seem to have a care in the world.

'So shall I show you the routine that I've come up with?' he said excitedly, whipping out a couple of sparkling, lilac-coloured ribbons from his basket and twirling them around his head.

'Yes, please,' Dotty and Orinthia chorused, and

once they had rounded up the rest of the household, everyone took their seats on the sofa ready for the performance. Peggy was less than impressed at having to forgo her weekend lie-in for a 'soppy old dance', but Suki, Bramwell and Caspian were downstairs in a shot, eager to support their brother. Grandy Brock came to watch too, as did Mrs Gastaldini, with Zuni the parrot perched on her shoulder.

Adjusting the needle on the gramophone, Kipling awaited the first bars of the piece of music. His routine began with a few graceful glides, but as the tempo quickened he began to pirouette and leap around the living room. Arms were flailed and feet were pointed, the layers of his tutu whirling and twirling around him like a shimmering pink Catherine wheel. Caspian couldn't help but join in, his nappy almost around his ankles as he jumped up and down to the jazzy melodies.

As the piece of music came to an end Kipling extended his leg into an arabesque, before finishing in a low curtsy.

Dotty and Orinthia looked at each other, almost speechless.

'So, what do you think?' Kipling said breathlessly. 'Did you like it?'

Orinthia didn't know what to say. The routine had no doubt been extremely impressive, but it would take a professional dancer at least a few months to master the intricate routine, let alone two retired cows! 'Kipling, that was . . . erm . . . amazing,' she said. 'Truly it was. But I think it might be a *little* complicated for Fosse and Falaise.'

'Oh,' said Kipling, obviously deflated. 'That was the simplified version.'

'How about we just teach the cows a couple of the easier steps?' Dotty suggested, obviously not wanting to hurt his feelings. 'Maybe a turn or two . . . and a couple of those bendy things?'

'You mean *pliés*?' said Kipling.

'Erm . . . yeah . . . pliés,' replied Dotty, obviously completely baffled by the ballet terminology. 'They were my favourite bit!'

Kipling, buoyed by Dotty's kind words, picked up his basket of props and headed straight for the front door. 'Well, what are you waiting for?' he said, pirouetting on to the porch. 'A director cannot keep his dancers waiting!'

By the end of the afternoon, thanks to Kipling's unwavering determination, Fosse and Falaise were able to trot into the middle of the enclosure and perform two continuous 360-degree turns. It hadn't been completely smooth sailing of course – there had been a couple of locked horns, and more than a few instances where the cows had wandered off in search of snacks – but little by little they'd mastered the first steps of the routine, and seemed to be really enjoying the challenge. Fosse had even started to nod her head as she walked, and Orinthia was convinced that Falaise was shaking her rump to the beat!

Kipling was equally delighted with his new protégées' progress. 'They'll be prima ballerinas by the end of the year,' he exclaimed as Dotty and Orinthia led the cows back to their stall for a well-deserved rest. 'Fosse would make a magnificent Sugar Plum Fairy in the *Nutcracker Suite*, and Falaise would be just brilliant in *Swan Lake*!

'Maybe we should get them to do a little practice performance in front of an audience before you and your mums head off to Norway, Dot?'

Dotty nodded. 'Sounds like a good idea to me. As long as you don't go inviting *everyone* in the village. Remember what I said about keeping our plans under wraps?'

Kipling smiled. 'Of course. Just our families and

Farmer Newing and . . . the artistic director of the Royal Ballet School perhaps?'

A stern look from Dotty silenced Kipling immediately and he let out a nervous laugh. 'Only joking!'

Dotty turned to Orinthia. 'What do you think, Rinthi? Are you up for putting on a little practice show?'

Orinthia nodded eagerly, excited at the prospect of showing Mum what they'd achieved. The worries she'd had about the nasty note left at the *Penny Lick* had now disappeared entirely, as she'd concluded that the threatening words *had* just been a silly joke. She reasoned with herself that she'd gone into panic mode, and cursed Mrs Pauncefoot and DI Snodgrass for causing her to react with such anxiety. But nothing could dampen her spirits now!

13

A few days later, and in preparation for Fosse and Falaise's test-run, Dotty, Orinthia and Kipling had set up a makeshift stage in the menagerie, similar to the one that the cows would be gracing at the Golden Udder Awards. They'd hung a large sheet of tarpaulin as a backdrop and put a table centre stage, where Orinthia would sit and act as the judge. As they didn't have a microphone stand they'd improvised by upending a large rake and placing it downstage, and they'd even hung a torch from the rafters to act as a spotlight!

Orinthia and Dotty couldn't wait to show their friends and families what they'd been working on. The choreography that Kipling had taught Fosse and Falaise was a sight to behold, and delivering the ice-cream cones to the judging table was now completely second nature to the cows – trotting around stage without so much as a nicker or a grunt.

'OK, it's nearly time to start,' said Kipling, as midday approached. 'Are we all ready?'

Dotty gulped. 'I'm so nervous. What if Fosse and Falaise don't listen to me? What if they get distracted? What if—'

'Dot, it's going to be fine,' Orinthia interrupted, putting a hand on her friend's shoulder. 'You've practised the routine a hundred times, if not more.'

'We believe in you,' Kipling reiterated. 'And so do the cows. You're going to be brilliant.'

Dotty took a deep breath. 'Thanks. I'm so glad I met you both.'

'Me too,' Orinthia replied, with warmth in her heart. 'This has been the best summer ever.'

As the clock struck twelve, the doors of the Mail-box Menagerie were opened to the guests, and they took their seats on the hay bales which had been arranged in curved rows, just like the stalls of a theatre. There was Mum and Séafra, Pem and Pandora, Grandy Brock and his children, and even Farmer Newing and his wife had shown up to offer their support. Poor Taber, still contagious with chickenpox, had been left at home with Uncle Max. All of the animails were watching too of course – Bettina the hippo from her mud bath, Petunia the octopus from her tank, and Geronimo and Gungho from their perches. Hanging upside down from the rafters, Titus the fruit bat undoubtedly had the best view in the house, albeit a topsy-turvy one!

'But where's Mrs Gastaldini?' Dotty asked, pointing to the empty seat next to Grandy Brock's. 'Is she not coming?'

'She had to take an important telephone call,' Grandy Brock replied. 'She won't be long, though, and said for you to make a start. She'll slip in when she can.'

Knowing that the telephone call was probably from Mrs Gastaldini's brother, Orinthia said no more, and once everyone had settled, Kipling took to the stage. He had changed into a white suit with a polka-dot bow tie, and had borrowed Grandy Brock's top hat, which was far too big for him and looked as if it might fall down over his face at any moment.

'Welcome everybody,' he bellowed into the rake microphone in his usual theatrical way. 'It's so nice to see you all here today. My friends and I have been working hard to bring you today's performance and it is my honour to present to you' – he gestured to Orinthia, who started a drum roll atop the judging table – 'the incredible, the inimitable, the irrepressible Fosse and Falaise! Enjoy the show!'

He took a bow and as the crowd broke into applause, he shuffled towards the wings. His introduction had been quite something, and Orinthia hoped more than anything that they weren't going to let down their audience!

The jazz music began, and on Dotty's command, the two cows trotted on to the stage. Fosse was carrying a huge strawberry cone in between her teeth, while Falaise had a knickerbocker glory balanced atop her head. Orinthia had been worried that they might be distracted by the spotlight, or get stage fright and stop for a poo, but the two cows remained remarkably focused.

They performed each of their choreographed moves without hesitation – zigzagging, stopping and turning with grace. (Or at least with as much grace as two 600 kilogram farm animals could muster!)

From her spot at the judging table, Orinthia watched the audience's reactions. The Brock children were leaning forward with their mouths open, full of peanut brittle, Farmer Newing's eyebrows were nearly at his hairline, and Pem was squeezing her wife's arm so tightly that Orinthia feared she might cut off her blood circulation.

After a couple more pliés it was time for Fosse and Falaise to deliver the ice creams to the judging table, and as a saxophone solo reached its crescendo, Dotty gave them their final command.

'OK, this is the home stretch . . .' Orinthia muttered to herself, suddenly feeling increasingly tense as the cows approached. 'You can do it, Fosse. You can do it, Falaise . . .'

The audience were on tenterhooks. For a moment it looked as if Falaise might turn back to the wings, and Orinthia felt her stomach lurch. The show had gone so well, they couldn't fall at the final hurdle! 'Come on, come on . . .' she whispered, trying to channel positive thoughts to the cow. 'Just bring me the ice cream cones . . .'

Thankfully, it seemed as though Falaise had picked up on her encouragement, and having parked herself parallel to the right-hand side of the table, the cow lowered her head and offered the strawberry cone to Orinthia like the most experienced of restaurant waitresses. With heart racing, Orinthia took it, before giving Falaise a much-deserved scratch behind the ears.

Fosse did just as good a job, coming to stand on the left-hand side of the table, so that the knickerbocker glory perched atop her head was in easy reach. Orinthia breathed a huge sigh of relief. They'd done it!

As the music faded, there was a huge cheer as the audience leapt to their feet in a standing ovation. Dotty, beaming with pride, took centre stage with a curtsy, before raising an outstretched arm to Fosse and Falaise, the way a conductor might do to an orchestra. Kipling and Orinthia joined her, the three of them hand in hand as they gave a final bow.

'Well done! Well done!' squealed Mum with delight, and Séafra had to pull her back in order to stop her from running on stage and throwing her arms around her daughter. Orinthia felt tears of happiness welling in her eyes. When Mum had been working at the car dealership she'd always been too busy to go and watch Orinthia perform in school plays or assemblies (come to think of it, she'd never even been to a parents' evening!). But now here she was, in the front row and beaming with pride.

'Well, what a dazzling display that was!' Grandy Brock stood up, turning to address the rest of the audience. 'Testament to the intelligence and wonder of our two bovine friends, and the relationships the children have built with them. What fantastic things creatures can do when treated with tenderness, respect and love. I've said it once and I'll say it again – a life without animals isn't a life worth living.'

There were shouts of 'hear, hear!' and 'well said!' from the audience, as they leapt up on stage to shower Dotty, Orinthia and Kipling with compliments.

Kipling grinned. 'The cows were better than any dancers I've ever seen before. So much passion, so much emotion, so much artistry!'

At that exact moment, as if lapping up the compliments, Falaise and Fosse edged forward and began to nudge Dotty playfully with their snouts, accompanied by some extra loud *moo*s.

'Oh, you want some treats, do you?' said Dotty. 'Well, I guess you both deserve some!' She took a handful of rolled oats from her pocket and offered them to the two cows, before asking Kipling to take them back to their enclosure for a well-deserved rest. Arm in arm with Orinthia, she looked to her two mums. 'So? What did you think? Will it go down well at the Golden Udder Awards?'

'I'm . . . I'm speechless!' said Pem. 'I had no idea you were working on something as impressive as this. And I'm so glad that I won't have to wear that awful ice lolly costume!'

The two women looked at each other and Pandora gave her wife a nudge. 'Go on, ask them.'

'Ask us what?' Orinthia and Dotty replied in unison.

'Well,' Pem began, 'Pandora and I were going to ask Mrs Gastaldini to man the *Penny Lick* while we were away in Bergen, but with her now heading off to Italy, we thought it might actually be wise for one of us to stay here and keep an eye on things.'

'So we were wondering,' continued Pandora, 'if Orinthia would like to take my spot, and join Dotty and Pem at the Golden Udder Awards this year?'

Orinthia's mouth slackened. 'You mean . . . go to Norway?'

Pandora nodded, her eyes twinkling.

'Oh my goodness, yes!' Orinthia squealed, throwing her arms around the two women. 'Yes, yes, yes!'

Dotty, whose mums had obviously been keeping the idea a secret from her too, looked equally as gobsmacked. 'This is the best news ever! We're going to have the most amazing time!'

Orinthia, bursting with joy, beckoned frantically to her mother, who was in the middle of chatting to Farmer Newing. 'Mum! Mum! Did you hear that? Pem and Dotty have asked me to go with them on their trip to Norway. Can I go? *Please?*'

Mum blinked, seemingly at a loss for words. 'Gosh, what a kind offer. And it's very lovely of them to invite you, but . . .' She swallowed. 'But I'm not sure, my darling. After everything that happened last year I don't know if I'm ready to let you out of my sight again just yet. Maybe in a few years, when you're a little older—'

'Please, Mum!' Orinthia pleaded, taking her mother's hand and squeezing it as hard as she could. 'Pem will look after me, won't you?'

'Of course I will,' she replied. 'You'll be in very safe hands. But it's your mum's decision to make, not mine. She knows what's best for you.'

Mum sighed heavily, deep in thought. Orinthia could understand why she was being so protective, but Norway wasn't very far away, and it wasn't like they'd be taking their journey by freight crate this time!

Orinthia gave her mum a pained stare. 'Please, Mum. I want to go so much. Dotty and I have been working so hard.' She batted her eyelashes. 'And poor Taber's still poorly – surely it'll be a relief for you to have one less child to look after for a few days?'

Mum let out a long, low sigh. 'If I say yes – and this is still entirely hypothetical – you must promise me, Orinthia, that you'll listen to everything Pem says and stay out of trouble.'

Orinthia nodded furiously. 'I promise.'

'There's no way that Mam will let us get up to any mischief,' added Dotty in support. 'She's ever so strict – she only lets me eat ice cream *once* a week. *Once* a week!'

Mum smiled, and obviously resigning herself to the fact that her daughter and Dotty weren't going to take no for an answer, said: 'OK, you may go.'

'Yes!' Orinthia exclaimed, grabbing Dotty by the hands and jumping up and down with glee. 'We're going to Norway! We're going to Norway!'

'But you better get packing fairly sharpish,' said Pem. 'We're leaving the day after tomorrow. We'll be taking the packet ship from London to Bergen.'

Orinthia blinked. 'Hang on, did you say we're going to Norway on board a *packet ship*?'

Pem nodded. 'That's right. The RMS *Mollusca*, I believe it's called.'

Orinthia couldn't believe her ears. 'That's the vessel Séafra and I stowed away on to get to New York last year!'

'Well I never!' said Pandora. 'Dotty's been telling us all about your adventures. You and your brothers are very brave, I must say. What's the ship like?'

'It's beautiful,' enthused Orinthia. 'There's first-class dining rooms, and lovely cabins and the views from the upper deck are incredible. Although, we were hiding down in the cargo hold for most of *our* journey, of course. But I made friends with the cabin boy, Mog. He's been promoted to deck cadet now, so hopefully this time he'll be able to give us a proper guided tour and—'

Just then Mrs Gastaldini burst through the front door of the menagerie. 'I'm sorry I'm late! I'm sorry I'm late!' she called out. 'Did I miss the performance?'

'I'm afraid you did,' Grandy Brock replied. 'And I'm not going to lie, Serafina, you missed out on quite the show.'

Mrs Gastaldini sighed. '*Peccato*. What a shame.'

'No matter,' said Grandy Brock reassuringly. 'Anyway, how is he?'

Mrs Gastaldini was seemingly confused, her face blank. 'Eh? How's who?'

'Your brother . . . in Italy. Was it not him you were talking to on the telephone?'

As realization hit, Mrs Gastaldini laughed and struck a hand to her forehead. '*Che sciocca che sono!* Silly me! He's feeling a little sorry for himself. We got chatting about things and time got the better of me, I'm afraid. Anyway, how was the *presentazione*? Did it all go as planned?'

'It went better than planned!' Orinthia exulted. 'And you're not going to believe it – Pem and Dotty have asked me to join them on their trip to Norway! I'm going to the Golden Udder Awards!'

Mrs Gastaldini gasped, doing a double take. 'You're . . . you're going to Bergen?'

Orinthia nodded, still not quite believing it herself.

'Well . . . how . . . lovely for you, Orinthia, but . . .' She paused, raising an eyebrow. 'Are you sure that's wise after last year's adventures? I'd hate for you to get into any trouble again. Especially so far away from home.'

Orinthia shook her head, tutting. 'You're just as bad as my mum! I'll be fine, I promise.'

Grandy Brock rubbed his hands together before

shouting out, 'Right! How about I go get us all some fish and chips for lunch? My treat! Who's hungry?'

'Meeeee!' was the unanimous reply, and everyone in the menagerie began to shout out their orders:

'I'll have a piece of cod please,' enthused Peggy.

'I'll have that too,' said Bramwell.

'Haddock!'

'Two saveloys!'

'A pickled egg!'

'Don't forget the mushy peas!'

Grandy was just about to reach into his breast pocket for pen and paper to take the order, when Kipling burst out of the cows' enclosure. 'Grandy, Grandy, come quick!' he exclaimed breathlessly. 'There's something wrong with Fosse and Falaise!'

14

Orinthia jerked to attention, her heart suddenly in her mouth. 'What do you mean, Kip? What's wrong with the cows?'

'Well . . . I took them into their stall like Dotty said and then they just went . . . limp. They're lying there now and aren't responding to anything. They can't pull themselves up.'

The menagerie suddenly erupted into panic.

'This is awful!'

'They were fine a minute ago!'

'How have they got sick?'

'Please say they won't die!'

'OK, OK, everyone needs to calm down!' said Farmer Newing, holding up an arm to quell the alarm. 'There's no need to panic. Animals get ill occasionally, just like us humans.' He turned to his wife. 'Mildred, could you go fetch my veterinary bag from the wagon? I'll go and take a look at them.'

She did, and within minutes everyone in the menagerie had piled into the cow enclosure. Fosse and Falaise looked in a terrible way, their heads lolling to the side and their black tongues hanging from their mouths. Dread clawed at Orinthia's insides, and she edged closer to Dotty, looping her arm through hers.

'Give them some space, and I'll do some checks,' said Farmer Newing, gesturing for the crowd to retreat a little. He dropped to his knees by the cows' sides, checking first their eyes, then their mouths, then their breathing.

'What's wrong with them?' whimpered Dotty, blanching. 'They look terrible.'

Farmer Newing looked up and pulled off his hat. 'I don't know yet, but I'm going to find out, don't you worry.' But the growing concern on the farmer's face was obvious. 'Mildred, pass me my stethoscope,' he ordered. 'I think I need to listen to their hearts.'

With every breath in the room held, Farmer Newing began his examinations. Orinthia began to panic. Had she and Dotty done something wrong? Had they been working the cows too hard? Had they collapsed with exhaustion?

'Well?' she pressed after a while. 'Do their hearts sound OK?'

Farmer Newing put down his stethoscope and was just about to answer, when all of a sudden Fosse pulled herself to her knees. She let out a loud retching sound and within the blink of an eye had proceeded to vomit all over the straw floor, splattering everyone's shoes in the process.

'*Yuuuuck!*' exclaimed the children, jumping backwards. 'Gross!'

Soon enough, Falaise followed suit, violently emptying her stomach and garnering even more disgusted reactions from all around her.

'Well, I think I know what the problem is here,' said Farmer Newing solemnly, shaking his head. 'Unfortunately, I think Fosse and Falaise have a severe case of *polyphagia extremus*.'

Despite the heat of the afternoon, Orinthia felt a chill tighten her skin. 'Oh no, that sounds awful!' she yelped, her shoulders starting to heave. 'They're going to die, aren't they? And it's all our fault!'

'There, there, it's OK, Orinthia,' Farmer Newing cut in, putting a reassuring arm around her. 'I'm sorry, I shouldn't have alarmed you. *Polyphagia extremus* simply translates as extreme overeating – gluttony! By the pink colour of their . . . regurgitations . . . these greedy cows have somehow managed to consume some of Mrs and Mrs Ambrose's strawberry ice cream. And rather a large amount by the look of it.'

'What? But how's that possible?' said Orinthia. 'Apart from the cones we used in the performance, we haven't let them near any ice cream.'

'And surely no one here would be foolish enough to feed ice cream to cows,' added Mrs Gastaldini. 'We all know better than to give sweets to animals. I think the cheeky things must have somehow found a tub and helped themselves.'

Fosse and Falaise looked to Orinthia and began to low as if in protest.

'It's no use trying to deny it,' Mrs Gastaldini replied, looking to the vomit on the floor with a raised eyebrow. 'The evidence is here for all to see.'

'See *and* smell!' said Kipling, covering his nose with his arm.

'I'm so sorry, Farmer Newing, we should have kept a closer eye on them,' said Dotty, on the verge of tears.

'Oh, it's no problem. These things happen. And they've eaten worse, trust me! Remind me to tell you the tale of the Christmas dinner fiasco another time. Cows and Brussels sprouts definitely don't mix!'

Dotty nodded sheepishly. 'They're going to be OK, though, aren't they?'

'Yes, yes,' the farmer replied. 'Nothing that a spoonful of my home-made Stomach-Soothing Elixir won't fix . . .' He reached into his bag and pulled out a large glass bottle. The cork stopper came out with a *pop*, and as he poured out a spoonful of lurid purple liquid, the cows began to whine. 'I'm sorry, ladies,' he said to them. 'But if you do the crime you must do the time. Now, open wide . . .'

'Do you think they'll be well enough to go to Norway?' asked Pem. 'It would be such a shame if we couldn't take them with us, especially after all the hard work the children have done with them.'

'I don't know, is the honest answer,' Farmer Newing replied, getting back up. 'We'll just have to wait and see.'

Orinthia ran a hand along Fosse's back, her mind racing. All of a sudden she couldn't help thinking back to the threatening note that had been left at the *Penny Lick*. Had Fosse and Falaise really helped themselves to the ice cream? Or had someone sneaked in and fed it to them, in an attempt to get them to pull out of the Golden Udder Awards? She felt a quiver in her tummy, and she couldn't help thinking once again that maybe the threat *had* been real after all.

Maybe she and Dotty should take another look at the note? See if they could work out whose handwriting it was? *Yes*, she'd ask her friend to bring it with her onboard the *Mollusca*, and perhaps they could solve the mystery before they reached Norway.

15

The evening before they were due to board the *Mollusca* for Norway, Orinthia was pacing the length and breadth of her bedroom, frantically deciding what to pack in her suitcase. Mum had brought up a tray of sandwiches for supper, and Séafra was perched on the end of the bed with an open copy of Ophelia Pearcart's diary. Orinthia had asked him to call out all of the things the intrepid explorer had packed for her round-the-world expedition. 'Walking boots . . .' he began. 'Jumper . . . raincoat . . . thick socks . . . sun hat . . . compass . . . camera . . . matches

. . . notebook and pen . . .'

The plan was that Orinthia would stay at Tupenny Mill that night, then Grandy Brock would take her, Fosse and Falaise to the port in his wagon the next morning to meet Dotty and Pem. All of this was dependent on how the two cows were feeling, of course. After another few doses of medicine, and a day relaxing in their enclosure listening to their beloved jazz, the cows *had* begun to perk up, but Farmer Newing still wasn't sure if they'd be well enough to make the trip. He would make a decision at the last minute.

As she gathered her belongings together, Orinthia began to daydream about the journey that lay ahead. She couldn't wait to see Mog again, and was even looking forward to seeing his dad, Captain Nelson Binnacle. The captain had been far from welcoming the last time their paths had crossed, but in his latest letter Mog had said that this definitely wouldn't be the case this time. Orinthia sincerely hoped so, but decided to pack a rubber ring, a length of rope and a torch just in case they needed to make a speedy escape overboard!

As such, it took all of Orinthia and Séafra's combined strength to push down and lock her bulging suitcase.

'Well, what did you expect, Rinthi?' said Séafra with a chuckle. 'Ophelia Pearcart was packing for year-long, cross-country expeditions, not a few days in Norway! I'm sure you don't need half of this stuff!'

Orinthia huffed, crossing her arms. 'Séafra, an explorer always needs—'

'—to be prepared!' her brother cut in, rolling his eyes as he finished the sentence he'd heard a million times before. 'I know that, Rinthi, but there's being prepared and there's not being able to physically lift your case from the ground.'

Orinthia wasn't going to back down, though, and once she'd managed to haul her suitcase downstairs it was time for her to head off to Tupenny Mill. 'Mum, Tabs, I'm off!' she said, popping her head around the living-room door.

Taber was lying on the sofa, his face still plastered in blotchy red spots. Even though he had a pile of comics to read and a huge bunch of grapes to nibble on, the poor thing looked so miserable. He sprang to his feet and turned to his sister. 'Awwww, I wish I could give you a cuddle before you go, Rinthi,' he said sadly. 'I'm going to miss you.'

A lump formed in Orinthia's throat. 'I'm going to miss you too, Tabs. But when I get back – and *if* you're a little less spotty – I'll give you the longest, loveliest, snuggliest cuddle you've ever had, I promise.'

Taber's face brightened momentarily, until he saw Mum standing in the doorway. 'Taber Shalloo, you know Doctor Badeel said that you need to be resting,' she barked. 'Get back on that sofa at once!'

The little boy reluctantly did as Mum said, blowing his sister a final kiss, before snatching up one of his comics in obvious frustration.

At the front door, Séafra and Mum huddled to say their goodbyes.

'*I'm* going to miss you too, you know,' said Séafra as Orinthia pulled on her coat. 'It's weird you going off on an adventure without me. I'm a little jealous.'

'Ha! I knew there was still a little bit of *explorer* left in you, Séafra Shalloo!' Orinthia replied, punching her brother playfully on the shoulder.

Séafra laughed. 'I wouldn't go *that* far!'

'And I don't think my nerves could handle the both of you going off again,' added Mum. She pulled Orinthia in close and when she finally let go, she had tears in her eyes.

'Aw, don't cry, Mum, I'm going to be fine!' said Orinthia.

'I know, I know,' Mum sniffed, reaching for a

hanky to dab her eyes. 'Have the best time, and be good. Look out for Dotty and listen to everything Pem says, OK?'

Orinthia nodded. 'I will.'

'And make sure you get an early night tonight. Fosse and Falaise included. I can't imagine that Mog will be too happy if he has to board two grumpy, sleep-deprived cows first thing tomorrow morning!'

Orinthia didn't know how on earth she was going to get an early night with all of the excitement coursing through her, but she promised Mum that she would nonetheless.

When she arrived at Tupenny Mill, the Brocks were just about to tuck into their evening meal and, even though she'd just eaten her weight in sandwiches at home, Orinthia thought it would be rude not to join them.

As she sat down, Mrs Gastaldini brought over a steaming bowl of *zuppa di verdure* – a chunky soup packed with vegetables and beans. It was her last night in the Mill too, as she would be travelling to Italy the following afternoon.

'So will you wake me up in plenty of time in the morning?' Orinthia asked Grandy Brock as they talked through the next day's itinerary. The RMS

Mollusca was due to set sail at eleven sharp, so they'd arranged to meet at the port at ten, to give them plenty of time to find Mog and board the cows. The drive was going to take a few hours so they would have to leave Little Penhallow just after dawn.

'I certainly will,' replied Grandy Brock, wiping his soup bowl clean with a crust of bread. 'I've set my alarm clock. Hasn't let me down in thirty years. Touch wood.' He knocked the side of his head as if it were made from solid oak and everybody laughed.

'I wish I was going with you too, Rinthi,' said Peggy with a huff.

'Me too,' said Kipling. 'You're going to have so much fun. It's not fair.'

The rest of Grandy Brock's brood, equally as forlorn, nodded in agreement.

'Now, come on, children, we've been through this,' said Grandy Brock. 'If you were to all go gallivanting off to Norway, then who'd help me keep the Mailbox Menagerie running, *hmm*? I'd leave Mr Malagasy in charge if I could, but something tells me he wouldn't take a managerial role very seriously . . .'

Grandy Brock nodded to the ring-tailed lemur, who was reclining on the top bookshelf, eating the remains of a very over-ripe banana while simultaneously breaking wind.

'Will you and Dotty bring us back some presents?' asked Kipling.

'We'll do one better than that,' said Orinthia with a huge grin. 'We'll bring back the Golden Udder and the cash prize!'

16

'Orinthia, quickly! Wake up! We've overslept!'

Orinthia lurched up, rubbing her eyes. Grandy Brock, fully dressed in his usual three-piece suit, was standing over her bed, his face panic-stricken.

'But . . . but I thought you set an alarm clock?' Orinthia groaned sleepily.

'I did,' Grandy Brock replied. 'Well, at least I thought I did. But for some reason it didn't go off. So you need to get up and dressed right away. If we don't leave soon we're not going to get to the port in time!'

'And are Fosse and Falaise allowed to come?' Orinthia asked.

Grandy Brock nodded. 'Yes, Farmer Newing has just left and has given them the all-clear. Now, get up, we need to leave in ten minutes!'

He hotfooted it out of the door and Orinthia quickly swung out of the blankets. She was more than happy when her alarm didn't go off on a school day, or when she had to go to an early morning dentist appointment, but today definitely wasn't the day to be sleeping in. As fast as she could, she leapt to where she'd left her clothes on the chair the night before, and began to get dressed. She slipped on a crisp checked summer dress with a rounded collar, and tied a cardigan around her waist. She'd wanted to brush her hair and wash her face, but there just wasn't time.

Rushing downstairs, she found the kitchen table laid for breakfast. There was toast in the rack, and Orinthia could smell sausages sizzling in a pan. Mrs Gastaldini was spooning tea leaves into an awaiting teapot. 'OK, Orinthia, sit down,' she said. 'Breakfast is almost ready.'

'Serafina, I've already said, we don't have time!' yelled Grandy Brock, pulling on his hat all a-fluster. 'If we don't leave immediately then we're going to miss the ship. We can have something when we arrive at the port.' He made a beeline for the front door, urging Orinthia to do the same.

'No, no, no!' Mrs Gastaldini insisted, striding forth and blocking Orinthia's path. '*Nessuno parte prima di fare colazione!* Nobody is leaving without eating a proper breakfast. It's the most important meal of the day. You should have checked your alarm clock properly, Amos.' She pulled out Grandy Brock's chair at the head of the table, her face stern. '*Siediti adesso!* Sit!'

'OK, OK,' said Grandy Brock reluctantly, holding up his hands in appeasement. 'But we can't be long.'

He and Orinthia wolfed down their sausages and toast as quickly as they could. It was unlike Orinthia not to enjoy a good breakfast, but she was so aware of missing the packet ship that there was no time to savour every mouthful – her food barely touched the sides.

As soon as she'd finished, she pushed back her plate and slurped the last of her tea. But Mrs Gastaldini was immediately by her side with the frying pan, trying to dish out a second helping. Orinthia knew that she meant well, and that Italians hated rushing, especially where mealtimes were concerned, but couldn't she see that they had to get going? Didn't she understand that if the *Mollusca* left without them they wouldn't make it to Norway in time for the awards?

Thankfully, Grandy Brock was more than aware of the predicament they were in and pushed back his chair. 'Serafina, I appreciate your kind hospitality, and on any other occasion I would have been over-joyed with another helping of sausages, but we really must leave. Now, I'll see you this evening before you depart for Italy.'

He got up, and without giving Mrs Gastaldini a chance to protest, he planted a kiss on her cheek, and he and Orinthia were finally out of the door. They jumped into the front cab of the rusty old wagon, and with Fosse and Falaise already settled in the back, they were on their way.

But time was going to be tight. The clock on the dashboard showed that it was already quarter past eight and it took at least two hours to get to London. There wasn't another packet ship leaving for Bergen for another few days, and by that time the competition would already be over. Orinthia couldn't sit still, adjusting and readjusting her position in her seat every few minutes. This was not the start to the day that she'd been hoping for.

With Little Penhallow behind them, the narrow windy roads were soon replaced with busy carriage-ways, thick with traffic. Orinthia looked out of the window, routinely checking every road sign they passed for the word *London*. But all of the place names were unfamiliar – *Bagenham*, *Upper Pangley*, *Chitterling-On-Sea*, *Lower Sharborough*, *Trimpton* . . .

'How long until we're there, Grandy?' she asked after an hour, as they passed the turning for a town called *Brightley-By-Thames*.

'Well, it shouldn't be long before we reach London,' he said, not taking his eye off the road. 'But it might take us a while to get across town. You know how busy the capital is, especially with it being a weekend. I'm not going to lie, Orinthia, I'm not sure if we're going to make it on time.'

Orinthia puffed out her cheeks and, resigning herself to the fact that all she could do was keep her fingers crossed and hope for the best, she closed her eyes. Even though she'd only been up for a few hours she already felt exhausted, and before long she'd drifted off to sleep . . .

17

When Orinthia next opened her eyes, Grandy Brock's wagon had come to a screeching halt. Still half-asleep and feeling a little disorientated, she looked up, squinting against the sun. Hang on a minute! Was that the horizon in the distance? And were they . . . boats?

'Have we arrived, Grandy?' she asked, as the old man pulled up the handbrake.

'Of course we have!' he replied. 'My foot wouldn't be off the gas if we were still en route, would it?' He yanked the key from the ignition and quickly unbuckled his seatbelt. 'Now, I'm going to find one of the deckhands to help me get Fosse and Falaise on board. You go and find Dotty and Pem.'

The noise was deafening as Orinthia stepped on to the port – the bellowing of the deckhands competing with the squawks of seagulls, and the blasts of foghorns overlapping the clamour of passengers making their way on board. Praying that it hadn't yet departed, Orinthia frantically looked around for the *Mollusca*, and to her delight, there it was, bobbing at anchor only a few metres away! It was just as magnificent as she'd remembered – its white paintwork gleaming and its three stout funnels already bellowing out steam.

But she didn't have time to stand about and reminisce. Pushing her way into the crowd of waiting passengers, Orinthia pulled herself on to her tiptoes to get a better view. There were men in suits and bowler hats, excitable children being pulled back by their parents, travellers laden with trunks, suitcases and holdalls . . .

All of a sudden she caught sight of a familiar flame-haired boy and her heart leapt. 'Mog!' she shouted, waving her arms to get his attention. 'Mog, over here!'

He turned, revealing a dungaree-clad girl and poofy-haired woman standing beside him. It was Dotty and Pem! Thank goodness they'd already found each other!

Orinthia pelted towards them through the throng of people. 'I'm so sorry for keeping you all waiting,' she gasped, catching her breath before pulling Dotty and Pem into a tight hug. Their relief was tangible.

'What happened?' asked Dotty. 'We thought you weren't coming.'

'Grandy Brock's alarm clock didn't go off and then Mrs Gastaldini wouldn't let us leave until we'd had breakfast and—'

'It's fine!' interrupted Mog, joining the huddle. 'You're here now, that's the main thing. And besides, you didn't think I'd let the *Mollusca* leave without you, did you? You're our guests of honour, after all!'

'Eh? What do you mean?' Orinthia asked, still panting.

'We're going to be travelling first class!' said Dotty, with a gleam in her eye. 'Mog's giving us one of the best cabins on the ship.'

'Really?' said Orinthia, not quite believing what she'd just heard.

Mog grinned. 'My way to apologize for the ghastly

way that my pa and the crew treated you last time you were on board. And Cook is preparing something extra special for you to eat tonight. Just you wait and see . . .'

'Oh Mog, thank you!' Orinthia squealed, throwing her arms around him, much to his embarrassment. 'And Captain Binnacle has agreed to it?'

'It was actually my idea,' came a gruff voice from above. 'In fact, it will be an honour to have you sail with us again. It's so wonderful to see you.'

Orinthia craned her neck and looked up.

Captain Binnacle was striding down the ship's gangway towards them, holding out a hand. He was every bit as impressive as Orinthia had remembered – dressed in a navy epauletted jacket, with his hair tumbling from beneath a tricorn hat.

For some reason, as her palm met with the captain's, Orinthia felt a little star-struck. Her tummy was all aflutter. 'It's . . . it's lovely to see you too,' she stuttered, her tongue suddenly feeling too big for her mouth. 'But what about Duffel and Drake? They're not still working on board the *Mollusca*, are they? I really don't want to cross paths with them again.'

Orinthia remembered Duffel and Drake all too

well. They were the two deckhands who had tied her and Séafra up last time they were on board. She shuddered, thinking of their calloused hands, bad breath and their intimidating squid tattoos.

'Don't you worry,' said Captain Binnacle, with a throaty laugh. 'Those two are long gone. They got caught leaving the Whiskered Kipper without paying for their pies and grog last month. Let's just say they felt the long arm of the law . . .'

Orinthia and Dotty looked to each other, sharing a sigh of relief.

'Anyway, I must ask you all to get on board now,' continued the captain, clapping his hands together. 'I want to set sail before that north wind starts to blow in.'

Pem nodded and picked up her suitcase. 'Now, have I remembered everything? Passport: check! Money: check! Ice cream: check! OK, I think we're good to go!'

'How are you transporting the ice cream?' queried Orinthia. 'Isn't it going to melt before we get to Norway?'

Dotty grinned. 'Remember that girl, Demelza, I was telling you about? The one who invented all the amazing machines for the creamery? Well, she came up with a portable freezer to slot into Mam's suitcase.

It should keep the ice cream nice and cold until we arrive in Bergen.'

'Genius!' Orinthia exclaimed.

Grandy Brock, who'd managed to safely board Fosse and Falaise and had just joined the gang at the dock, leant in to give them all a goodbye hug. 'Have a brilliant, brilliant time,' he said, squeezing Orinthia especially tight. 'But don't forget to do exactly as Pem says. I know your mum wants you on your best behaviour.'

Orinthia nodded, unexpected tears welling in her eyes. Grandy Brock had become somewhat of a father figure to her and her brothers over the past few months, and she was going to miss him. With suitcases in hand, she, Dotty and Pem made their way to the bow of the top deck, ready for the ship's departure. Last time she was on board, Orinthia had missed the excitement of setting sail, because she and Séafra had been forced to lay low in the cargo hold. This time, she had a prime view.

Dotty, who had never been to the capital before, began waving goodbye to the London skyline. 'Goodbye buses . . .' she called out. 'Goodbye big cathedral . . . goodbye lamp posts . . . goodbye smoky chimneys . . . goodbye huge tower thing with a clock . . .'

'That huge tower with a clock is called Big Ben,' said Pem. 'It's the most accurate timepiece in the world. And look –' she pointed to the big hand, which was reaching twelve – 'it's time to set sail.'

As the clock chimed the hour, the packet ship began to drift away and soon enough it was chugging through the waves with the city getting smaller and smaller by the minute. Orinthia felt her tummy turn with excitement. They were on their way to Norway!

18

The first afternoon aboard the *Mollusca* was spent in a flurry of exploration. While Pem opted to relax with a pot of tea on one of the terraces, Mog took the girls on a guided tour of the ship. Orinthia was over-joyed to be on board again, even if the rocking and rolling of the deck was taking a bit of getting used to!

'Wow!' said Dotty, looking around starry-eyed. 'The size of it is incredible!'

'Nearly three hundred metres long,' Mog replied. 'It's a bit of a maze and passengers are always getting lost. Last week I found a man looking for his bed in the engine room. And another time I had to stop an old lady from walking overboard in the middle of the night thinking that she was on her way to the toilet!'

'Oh dear, imagine sitting down for a piddle and finding yourself at the bottom of the ocean!' laughed Dotty. 'Gives a whole new meaning to the word seaweed! Get it? Sea-*weed*!'

The others groaned.

'How's your promotion to deck cadet?' Orinthia asked Mog as they made their way past the Turkish baths.

'Good,' Mog replied proudly. 'It's so much better than being a cabin boy. But they do work me hard . . .' He looked at his wristwatch. 'In fact, I should probably be getting back to my evening duties down in the engine room. Enjoy your dinner tonight. I'll see you both tomorrow morning?'

The two girls nodded, and Mog scampered off, leaving them to make their way back to their cabin. They were just passing the ship's grand staircase when a moustachioed man in a bowler hat came dashing down the corridor from behind him. '*Excusez-moi, excusez-moi!*' he called out, holding up a silver-tipped walking cane. He spoke with a squeaky French accent and was dressed ready for dinner in a black swallow-tail coat with peaked lapels, complete with a white cravat and cummerbund. 'Are you on your way to compete in zee Golden Udder Awards, *par chance*?' he asked.

'Yes,' Dotty replied. 'We're the British entrants.'

'Ah! I thought so! You are part of zee Ambrose family, *oui*? I 'ave 'eard so much about your mothers' new ice cream van. It looks *très* impressive.'

'Erm . . . thank you,' said Dotty. 'And *you* are?'

The man struck his forehead with his hand. 'I am so sorry, allow me to introduce myself,' he said, adjusting his hat. 'I am Monsieur Dubois, chairman of zee French Society of Ice Cream Enthusiasts.'

'So you're going to the Golden Udder Awards too?' Orinthia asked.

The man cleared his throat. '*Oui*. I get to travel a lot with my work, I am ever so lucky. I 'ave spent the past few weeks in England, and now I get to voyage to Norway on zis marvellous vessel. I have a lovely cabin overlooking zee Palm Court.' He smiled. 'You both must be very excited to be competing?'

Orinthia and Dotty nodded.

'And where in Bergen are you staying, may I ask?' said Monsieur Dubois.

'A local farmer has agreed to put us up in his

farmhouse in the mountains,' Dotty replied.

'How wonderful!' Monsieur Dubois reached into the inner pocket of his suit jacket and pulled out a small notebook and pen. 'And what time are you competing on zee day? I always like to know the schedule.'

Dotty scratched her head in thought. 'Erm . . . sometime mid-afternoon, I think.'

'*Magnifique,*' replied Monsieur Dubois, making a quick note. 'I am sure you will 'ave a wonderful time onstage with your cows.' He smiled and quickly looked to the large clock hanging at the top of the staircase. 'Ah! *Est-ce le moment?* I best get going. I want to catch zee sunset up on deck before dinner.'

'We're dining in the first-class salon this evening!' Orinthia boasted, pushing back her shoulders with pride. 'We're friends of Captain Binnacle, you see.'

'Very impressive,' Monsieur Dubois replied with a nod of admiration. 'Well, it was lovely to meet you, Orinthia . . . Dotty, *enchanté.* No doubt I will see you again before we reach dry land.'

The man toddled off in the direction that he'd just come, his cane *tap-tapping* against the floorboards as he went.

He'd disappeared out of sight when, all of a

sudden, something occurred to Orinthia. Her posture spiked and a sickening feeling started to well in her tummy. She whipped round to face Dotty.

'Dot, how did that man know my name?' she asked urgently.

'Eh?' said Dotty, looking puzzled. 'What do you mean?'

'Monsieur Dubois! He said: *very nice to meet you, Orinthia*. But I hadn't introduced myself.'

Dotty shrugged. 'I dunno, Rinthi. You must have slipped your name into the conversation at some point, I guess?'

Orinthia was pretty sure that she hadn't. And as she mined the details of the conversation, something else occurred to her, making her stomach lurch once more. 'Dotty, he also said that he was sure that we'd have *a wonderful time onstage with our cows*. But how did he know about Fosse and Falaise? I haven't told anyone about our plans, have you?'

'No, of course not,' said Dotty, tugging at her plaits. She gulped as realization hit her. 'How on earth did he find out about them?'

Orinthia crossed her arms decisively. 'It's obvious, isn't it? He's been spying on us!'

'Spying?' Dotty spluttered. 'Why?'

Orinthia glanced across the landing to check that they weren't being watched, then brought her voice down to a whisper. 'Think about it. Monsieur Dubois is from France so he's *obviously* going to want the French ice cream makers to win at the Golden Udder Awards. And if he's heard about your mums' amazing reputation, and thought they might be a threat, then . . .'

'. . . then he might be trying to sabotage our chances of taking home first prize!' finished Dotty, her breath hitching. '*He* could have been the one that left the vicious note in the *Penny Lick*! And the one that fed all that strawberry ice cream to Fosse and Falaise!'

Orinthia nodded forlornly. 'Exactly. He did say that he'd been in England for the past few weeks, after all. He could have come to Little Penhallow!' She only had to think back to Mrs Pauncefoot and DI Snodgrass to know the lengths to which some grown-ups would go to get what they wanted – they'd kidnapped Taber and held him hostage and . . . well . . . it didn't bear thinking about what else they might have done, if she and Séafra and the pelicans hadn't come to his rescue.

Dotty gasped. 'Oh my goodness! What if he tracks

us down in Norway? What if he harms us? Or Mam?' Her face fell into her hands in a flurry of panicked sobs.

'Hey, hey, it's OK, Dot,' said Orinthia, putting an arm around her friend's heaving shoulders. 'We're safe while we're on the *Mollusca* with Mog and Captain Binnacle. And we didn't give him the address of where we're staying. But we do need to find out what Monsieur Dubois is up to, and put a stop to it!'

Dotty ran a hand through her hair. 'But how?'

Orinthia thought for a moment and soon a plan was coming together in her mind. 'Didn't Monsieur Dubois say that he was on his way to watch the sunset on the top deck?'

'Yes,' Dotty nodded.

'Which means that at this very moment in time . . . his cabin is empty.'

Dotty's eyes widened as she grasped what Orinthia was implying. 'But how do we know which cabin is his?'

'Don't you remember? He said it overlooked the Palm Court. Now come on, let's go.'

19

The two girls took an oblique route through the ship to Monsieur Dubois' cabin, creeping through narrow passages and corridors where they would be less likely to be spotted – Mog's tour and Orinthia's knowledge of the ship were coming in very handy! They slipped through the saloon deck, where a busy clatter of pans and voices was coming from the galley, then across the Palm Court to a set of stairs leading to a landing above. Looking over their shoulders to check that they weren't being watched, Orinthia and Dotty raced up the steps and came to a door marked with the number twelve.

'OK, I think this is his cabin,' whispered Orinthia, jostling nervously from foot to foot. 'Logistically this is the only one that can have a view over the Palm Court.'

'But how are we going to get in?' asked Dotty, rattling the door handle and unsurprisingly finding it locked.

'Good question,' Orinthia replied, having not thought that far ahead. She looked around and, on seeing a cleaner exiting another cabin at the end of the corridor, called out in her poshest and most innocent-sounding voice. 'Erm . . . excuse me. I wonder if you can help? My sister and I seem to be locked out of our cabin. Our mamma is relaxing on the terrace and we really don't wish to disturb her. Could you possibly let us in? We need to get changed for dinner.'

The cleaner hurried towards them. 'Of course,' she said, reaching for the brass master key hanging at her waist. She unlocked the door and pushed it open. 'There you go. Enjoy the rest of your evening.'

As she departed, Dotty and Orinthia shared a smug look, and not wanting to waste any more time, the two girls crept inside.

The cabin was dark apart from a small slither of

sunset streaming in through the porthole, highlighting everything in an eerie orange light.

'Hello?' Orinthia whispered, checking that they were alone.

When no reply came, she groped her way through the dark and pushed the mahogany desk chair up against the door so that they could not be surprised.

The two girls looked around, wondering where to start their search for any clues to Monsieur Dubois' plans.

Orinthia headed to the large four-poster bed, her fingers creeping beneath its crisp linen sheets. She felt around, hoping that Monsieur Dubois might have concealed something there, but she found nothing apart from a cold hot-water bottle and a pair of bed socks. Dotty riffled through the drawers of the desk, but she too found nothing of any use.

'Let's check his luggage,' whispered Orinthia, heading to the two leather suitcases propped up against the wardrobe. She dropped to her knees, but just as she was unfastening the first clasp, a loud knock sounded at the door, causing the chair barricade to rattle.

The two girls jumped and Orinthia felt her heart quickening.

'Monsieur Dubois?' came a gravelly voice from

outside. 'A phone call has come through for you from Norway. Would you like to come and take it?'

The door handle turned and Orinthia froze. It was Captain Binnacle!

'Monsieur Dubois, are you in there?' the captain pressed.

'Erm . . . *oui, oui!*' she quickly replied, mimicking Monsieur Dubois' French accent as best she could. 'Don't come in, I'm . . . erm . . . just getting out of zee bath. I shall take zee call shortly . . .'

'No problem. Just make your way to the ship's radio room. Do you know where it is?'

Orinthia swallowed. '*Oui, oui.* Thank you, Captain. *Merci.*'

There was an uneasy silence as Captain Binnacle walked away, and it was only when the sound of his heavy footsteps had completely dissipated that Orinthia let out a long sigh of relief. Nonetheless, she knew that it was time for her and Dotty to be making a quick exit. She gestured to her friend to get up, and they slipped out of the cabin as quietly and as clandestinely as they'd entered.

'*Oooosh*, that was close,' said Dotty as they slunk down the staircase back towards the Palm Court. 'I know that Captain Binnacle is your friend now, but breaking into someone else's cabin would surely warrant walking the plank!'

Orinthia nodded, adrenalin coursing through her like an electrical current.

'Your French accent was brilliant, though!' added Dotty, with a playful nudge. 'I could never have improvised so well. All that *oui, oui* and *merci*!'

Orinthia smiled. 'Kipling's theatrical ways must have rubbed off on me. If my exploring career doesn't work out, maybe I'll have a home on the stage.'

Still shaken by their close call, the two friends rounded the corner to their own sleeping quarters at speed, just in time to find Pem coming out of the cabin. She was dressed for dinner in a full-skirted cocktail dress, with her bouffant hair falling loose around her shoulders. 'Ahh, there you are!' she exclaimed. 'I was wondering where you two had got to. Was just about to send out a search party!'

The girls shared a guilty look.

'Erm . . . sorry, Mam, there was just so much to see,' lied Dotty, shiftily averting her gaze. 'We got distracted.'

Pem raised an eyebrow. 'Well, go and get changed. It's nearly time for dinner. We don't want to be late.'

20

At eight o'clock a gong sounded, signalling that it was time for dinner. Dressed in their best clothes, Pem, Dotty and Orinthia made their way through the RMS *Mollusca* to the first-class dining room. Following their encounter with Monsieur Dubois, Orinthia was feeling more than a little apprehensive about leaving the safety of their cabin, and unusually for her, wasn't feeling very hungry. Dotty was obviously feeling the same, walking silently at her mother's side like a beefy bodyguard.

'You two are very quiet this evening,' said Pem.

'Everything all right? Nothing bothering you, is there?'

Dotty flinched as if she'd been caught red-handed doing something naughty. 'What? Oh . . . no, everything's fine, Mam. We're just a bit tired, that's all.'

She glanced to Orinthia to back up her story, who immediately jumped in with, 'Yeah, it's been such a long day. Travelling is *soooo* tiring.'

Pem smiled. 'Well, it'll be early nights all round then. A quick dinner then bed for us all.'

At the entrance to the dining room, the trio were greeted by a waiter in a white shirt and black bow tie, and Orinthia was suddenly reminded of the similar penguin-like outfit that she had worn as a disguise when she was last on board. It had been horribly itchy, and she was glad to be wearing a cool cotton blouse and skirt this time round.

'Good evening,' said the waiter, dipping his head in welcome. 'My name is Luca and I'll be looking after you this evening. Please, follow me, you shall be dining at the top table.'

Orinthia and Dotty looked at each other in delight. The top table? How fancy!

Luca led them through the dining room, and Orinthia marvelled at the elegance of the place. It was panelled in polished mahogany, with ornamental carvings highlighted with gold leaf. Leaded-glass windows obscured the portholes, and alcoves were lit by twinkling crystal lamps. So different to the damp, dingy cargo hold of last year's voyage!

'Here we are,' said Luca, as they arrived at a grand circular table at the far end of the room. It had been laid with a crisp linen tablecloth and had a beautiful vase of fresh flowers at its centre. Luca handed each of them a leather-bound book, adorned with a red tassel. 'Here are the menus. Any questions, don't be afraid to ask.'

As they sat down, Orinthia was shocked by how much cutlery had been set at each place – there were knives and forks of all shapes, and spoons of all sizes. How was she going to know which one to use, and when?

When the first course arrived, Orinthia couldn't believe her eyes. It was an opulent seafood platter, presented on a bed of ice and served with wedges of lemon. There were lobster and prawns, oysters and mussels, not to mention ribbons of smoked salmon and terrines of potted shrimp. As Orinthia's appetite returned with a vengeance, all thoughts of Monsieur Dubois seemed to disappear.

Having tucked their napkins into their collars as the rest of the diners were doing, the trio dived in. Dotty especially enjoyed cracking open the crab claws and picking out the sweet pink meat, all the while pretending to be a carnivorous kraken of the deep. 'Surrender, little crustacean!' she bellowed. 'I want you in my belly!'

Orinthia had never tasted food so yummy. Even though Mum's cooking had improved a lot since she'd invested in some cookbooks, this was in a completely different league. It was all that she could do to stop herself picking up her plate and licking it clean!

'Isn't this posh?' said Pem, looking around in awe. 'Fine food, chandeliers, silver cutlery . . . I feel like Marie Antoinette!' She thought for a moment. 'Before she had her head cut off, of course!'

The children laughed.

When the main course arrived it was equally as breathtaking; juicy roast duckling was accompanied by apple sauce and served with buttered greens and creamed carrots. Dessert was the ship's famous Pineapple Royale – a glistening dome of wobbly orange jelly, decorated with crowns of whipped cream and topped with cherries. With what she hoped was the right spoon, Orinthia plunged into it with a satisfying *squelch* – it was like delving into the loveliest of gifts!

But something suddenly caught Dotty's eye, causing her spoon to drop from her grasp. It fell on to her plate with a noisy clatter, and her face turned ashen. When Orinthia turned to see what she was looking at, she soon realized why – Monsieur Dubois was standing in the entrance to the dining salon, waiting to be seated! Orinthia gasped, and as his eyes met with hers, she felt her heart pounding in her chest. But instead of acknowledging that he'd seen her, the moustachioed Frenchman quickly averted his gaze as if they'd never met.

He obviously doesn't want Pem to know what he's up to, Orinthia thought to herself. *What a sly thing.*

She and Dotty watched as Luca escorted him to a table tucked away in the corner of the dining room, as far away from theirs as physically possible. Once seated, he took out the little notebook and pen from his breast pocket once more, placing it down on the table within easy reach. He was obviously planning on spying and making more notes about them, and Orinthia had to stop herself from getting up and snatching it away from him.

'Girls, what is it?' asked Pem, looking in the direction of Monsieur Dubois' table, puzzled. 'What are you looking at?'

'It's . . . erm . . . nothing, Mam,' Dotty replied curtly, before quickly pushing back her chair. 'I need to use the bathroom, that's all.' She stood up and looked to Orinthia with urgency. 'You need to go too, right Rinthi?'

Orinthia didn't, but suspecting her friend had an ulterior motive for wanting to leave the table, she nodded and put down her cutlery. 'We won't be long, Pem.'

The two slipped out of the dining room, and it quickly became clear that Orinthia's suspicions had been correct – her friend hadn't needed to use the bathroom at all. Dotty pulled her into the shadows of a nearby vestibule, bringing her voice down to a whisper. 'We told him where we were dining earlier,' she said, panicked. 'So he obviously saw it as an opportunity to do some more snooping.'

Orinthia nodded. 'And did you notice how he looked away when I caught his eye? He blatantly didn't want your mam to know that he'd spoken to us.'

'We need to make sure that he doesn't follow us back to our cabin after dinner,' said Dotty. 'The last thing we need is him locking us in so we can't leave the ship in the morning.'

Orinthia blanched at the thought. 'Good idea. Let's go back to the table, make an excuse about being too full to finish our Pineapple Royales, then leave while he's still eating. He's *not* going to sabotage our chances of winning!'

Back in the dining room, Pem had finished her Pineapple Royale and was sitting back with satisfaction. 'That was delicious,' she said, wiping the corners of her mouth. 'Yum yum!'

The girls smiled tentatively, but didn't sit back down.

Pem's brow furrowed. 'What are you waiting for? Get stuck in before the waiter clears your desserts away.'

Orinthia shot a quick glance to Monsieur Dubois who, much to her dismay, was already receiving his main course. They had to get out of here, and fast!

'I think we're actually a bit too full to finish our desserts, Mam,' said Dotty. 'Can we just go back to the cabin?'

Pem's eyes widened, her face looking as if she'd just been given the most incredible news. 'My daughter, too full for pudding? Ha! Well, that's a first!'

'I think we both ate a few too many of those crab claws earlier on,' said Orinthia with a nervous laugh.

'Back to the cabin it is then,' said Pem with a chuckle. 'But you wait until Mum hears that you said no to a sweet treat, Dotty! She's never going to believe it.'

She got up, and the trio headed to the doorway. But as Pem made her way out, Orinthia noticed that Dotty had hung back. She was at Monsieur Dubois' table, pointing something out to him through the nearby porthole. He turned to look, and as he did Dotty seized her chance – pilfering the Frenchman's notebook from the table and stuffing it into her pocket.

'Come on, Dotty!' called Pem from the doorway. 'No dilly-dallying! I thought you said you needed an early night.'

'Coming, Mum!' Dotty replied, and she quickly bid farewell to Monsieur Dubois before turning on her heel with a proud grin on her face.

21

It was midnight, and with Pem finally fast asleep, the two girls hunkered down in the bottom bunk to study the pages of the stolen notebook under the pale light of Orinthia's torch. Dotty brought out the threatening note that had been left at the *Penny Lick*, and with a bit of comparing, it didn't take them long to realize that the two sets of handwriting were exactly the same!

Orinthia felt her breath quicken. 'It's a match! The lettering is identical!' she whispered, pointing to the scrawled inky writing. The *y*'s have the same long straight line, and the *o*'s are really small. Even the ink is the same shade of blue.'

'It's the proof that we needed,' Dotty replied urgently. 'It's just too much of a coincidence that Monsieur Dubois knew your name and knew about Fosse and Falaise. And now this! He *did* come to Little Penhallow. He *has* been spying on us.'

Orinthia pulled the blankets up to her ears – she didn't want Dotty to see the sheer terror that was no doubt plastered across her face. 'We need to make a plan for when we reach Norway tomorrow morning,' she said, trying to keep her voice level. 'No doubt Monsieur Dubois will try and follow us to the farm. We somehow need to stop him from disembarking, so we can make a getaway from the ship without being spotted.'

Dotty nodded, quickly checking that her mum was still asleep. 'But how are we going to do that?'

Orinthia thought for a moment. Could they hide in the cargo hold once the ship had moored and wait for Monsieur Dubois to disembark, perhaps? No, Pem would be worried sick if she thought they were missing. What about if they barricaded Monsieur Dubois in his cabin? No, that would be completely irresponsible.

'What about Mog?' suggested Dotty. 'Maybe he could lend a hand? Didn't he help you and Séafra make your escape from the *Mollusca* last time?'

Orinthia's lips parted at the idea, and she had to stop herself yelping out with glee. 'That's a brilliant idea, Dot. Mog knows the ship better than anyone. He'll know what to do. We'll go find him first thing in the morning.'

Dotty nodded, and having given her friend the quietest of high fives, Orinthia scampered up to her own bunk and clicked off her torch.

Morning came, bringing the Scandinavian coastline with it. After a breakfast of pastries and fresh fruit, it was time to get ready to disembark. As much as Dotty and Orinthia had been desperate to go and talk to Mog about their proposed plan, Pem hadn't given them a moment's privacy all morning. So they readied their luggage as quickly as possible and headed up to the top deck, under the pretence that they were going to say goodbye to Mog and Captain Binnacle.

With the wind in their hair, they ran to the bow of *Mollusca*. Up ahead, Bergen was coming into view, its port bathed in dazzling sunlight. Usually, Orinthia would have taken a moment to enjoy the scenery, but she knew she and Dotty didn't have much time. They *had* to find Mog as soon as possible and ask him to stall Monsieur Dubois!

Luckily for them, good fortune was on their side, and it wasn't long before they spotted the red-headed boy up in the crow's nest.

'Good morning, ladies,' he said, tipping an imaginary hat as he climbed down one-handed. 'Did you sleep well? Was the cabin to your satisfaction?'

'It was great, thanks,' Orinthia replied, perhaps a little too abruptly. 'But we need to ask you something, Mog. We need your help!'

The boy's brow furrowed. 'Oh dear, you're not in trouble again, are you? You don't need to make another escape in a freight crate?'

'No,' Orinthia replied. 'But it's really important. Now listen up . . .' She quickly relayed to Mog what had happened in the dining room the previous night, and her and Dotty's theory about Monsieur Dubois' intentions. 'And that's why we need to try and stall him. Do you think you can help us?'

Mog puffed out his cheeks. 'There's certainly never a dull moment when you're on board, Rinthi! Does trouble follow you around or do you just go chasing it?' He raised an eyebrow and Orinthia felt her heart sink. Now that Mog was a deck cadet, was he going to be unwilling to lend a hand? Would it be too much of a risk for him to help her once again?

She needn't have worried. A huge grin spread across Mog's face and he tapped the side of his nose. 'Leave it with me.'

22

Although Orinthia had no idea what Mog was planning, she knew that he could be trusted, and as the RMS *Mollusca* was piloted to shore, all she and Dotty could do was pray that he'd come good on his word.

Pem had joined them up on deck, and the trio sat on their upturned suitcases, watching as Bergen drew closer and closer. In the port, fishing boats were bobbing at anchor, their ropes criss-crossed like the lines of an etching. Along the quayside, rows of higgledy-piggledy wooden townhouses stood gable to gable – their cladding stained in shades of white, yellow and rust. And behind them, a range of craggy, verdant mountains rose up, their peaks disappearing into the clouds.

'Look! I can see a Norwegian flag!' said Pem, spotting the bright red banner with its blue-and-white cross flying at mast on the dock.

'And can you see that?' said Dotty, pointing out the two bottle-green carriages travelling up an impossibly steep hillside. 'They look like flying cars!'

'That's the Fløibanen Funicular,' said Pem. 'My guidebook says that the carriages go right to the top of the mountain. I bet there's some incredible views from up there.'

'Oh, there certainly are,' came an unexpected voice from behind. 'I took my entire family in one, the last time we visited Bergen.'

The trio turned and Orinthia had to suppress a yelp.

Monsieur Dubois was looming over them, pressing down on to his walking cane. Once again, he stood rigid in a firmly pressed suit and bowler hat.

'*Bonjour*, girls,' he said with a saccharine smile. 'Glorious morning, is it not?'

Orinthia and Dotty looked to each other in panic, neither answering. What was Monsieur Dubois doing up on deck? Why hadn't Mog stalled him?

'Girls, aren't you going to answer the gentleman?' asked Pem. 'Where are your manners?'

'Oh, do not worry,' he replied with a chuckle. 'I am sure they are just distracted by zee wonderful views.' He extended a hand to Pem, but Orinthia noticed that he didn't give her his name. After all, if he introduced himself as the chairman of the French Society of Ice Cream Enthusiasts, then no doubt she would question him further.

Orinthia was just about to suggest that they move to the aft, when Captain Binnacle appeared and tapped Monsieur Dubois firmly on the shoulder. 'Excuse me, sir, could I have a word?' he asked.

Monsieur Dubois balked. 'Erm . . . well, *bien sûr*, Captain. Although may I ask what about? We are just about to disembark, after all.'

'I just need to go through a discrepancy with regard to your passport. It won't take long.'

'But . . . but that is preposterous!' said the Frenchman, his voice rising sharply. 'There . . . there is nothing wrong with my passport!'

Despite his tone, Captain Binnacle didn't flinch. 'As I said, it won't take long. Shall we go to my office?' He held out a hand towards the nearby stairwell, and with a loud huff, Monsieur Dubois picked up his suit-cases and followed him downstairs.

Dotty and Orinthia looked at each other and smiled, suspecting that the arrival of Captain Binnacle had been Mog's doing. Hopefully he'd keep the Frenchman talking long enough so that they could leave the ship without him following them.

'I knew Mog would think of something,' whispered Orinthia, leaning into her friend and breathing a sigh of relief. 'I knew he'd come up with a good plan—'

'What was that?' asked Pem, turning to her daughter.

'Oh . . . oh nothing, Mam,' Dotty retorted quickly. 'Orinthia was just wondering . . . what's the plan now?'

'Well, as soon as we get off the ship we need to keep an eye out for Herr Larsen, our Norwegian host. He said that he'd meet us at the port and take us up to the farm.' She turned back towards the stairwell. 'I do hope that gentleman resolves the issues with his pass-port. Maybe we should see if Herr Larsen can give him a lift to wherever he's going in Bergen—?'

'NO!' Dotty cut in. 'I mean . . . I think we should get Fosse and Falaise to the farm straight away.

They'll be ever so tired after all the travelling.'

'Yes, you're probably right,' Pem replied. She picked up her suitcase, and as the ship's horn blew for the final time, Orinthia felt that she could finally relax. Monsieur Dubois was out of the picture.

23

With suitcases in hand, the trio headed down the gangway, and Orinthia was relieved to have her feet on dry land once more. The quayside was buzzing – fishermen were bringing in the morning's catch; hawkers selling lingonberry waffles and potato pancakes were calling out from their covered stalls; and a queue was already forming at the base of the Fløibanen Funicular. It was so different to the port in London – fresher, somehow, brighter.

'*God morgen!*' came a sudden voice from up ahead. '*Velkommen til Norge!* Welcome to Norway!'

Orinthia looked up to find a tall, thickset man with a beard as bushy as a hedgerow striding towards them through the crowds. He looked as if he had the DNA of a Viking mixed with that of a bear! He was wearing a russet wool suit with a large straw hat, and was pulling an empty wooden cart, its wheels clattering across the cobbles.

'Hello,' said Pem, looking up. 'Herr Larsen?'

'Yes, but please, call me Axel,' said the man, grabbing Pem's hand and shaking it so vigorously that Orinthia thought her arm might be pulled from its socket. 'You must be my British guests?'

'We are indeed. My name's Pem . . . this is my daughter Dotty . . . and this is our family friend, Orinthia.'

'Lovely to meet you all,' said Herr Larsen, revealing a big gap where one of his two front teeth was missing.

With the wind in her hair, Pem turned back towards the RMS *Mollusca*, where passengers were disembarking. 'We also have our two cows with us. I'm hoping that you might help us bring them up from the cargo hold?'

'No need,' Herr Larsen replied. 'I've already arranged for my farmhand to collect them and drive them up to the farm in our livestock trailer. They can bed down in one of the barns with my own animals once they arrive. Now, shall we start walking?' He clapped his hands together and turned to the mountain behind them. There was a winding pathway leading towards its craggy summit, which was barely visible through the clouds.

'Wait . . . we're *walking*? All the way up *there*?' said Dotty, looking up the steep ascent with incredulity.

'Of course!' said Herr Larsen. 'It's only a few kilometres! Now let's get going.'

With their luggage stacked in a precariously high tower atop Herr Larsen's cart, the party set off, and soon the winding pathway through the mountains had taken them around a glistening turquoise lake. It was perfectly flat – the surrounding peaks reflected in its waters as if it were a looking-glass.

'This is Fjærlandsfjorden,' said Herr Larsen, holding out an arm. 'A *fjord* is a long strip of sea between hills or mountains. We have many of them here in Norway, but this is undoubtedly one of the most beautiful.'

'Oooh, can we swim?' said Orinthia, jumping up and down excitedly, looking ready to pull off her clothes.

'You can if you want a frostbitten bottom!' said

Herr Larsen with a guttural laugh. 'Even in the summer the water is still very cold.'

Eager to capture the fjord's beauty, Orinthia reached into her satchel. Ophelia Pearcart had documented every one of her 200 expeditions in great detail by sketching everything she saw in pen and ink. Orinthia was keen to do the same, albeit using a film camera that Grandy Brock had lent her. She removed the lens cap and looked through the viewfinder. When she was happy with her composition she twizzled the focus-ring until the image was pin-sharp, and with a *click-clack* she pressed the shutter, immortalizing the wonderful scene. She couldn't wait to develop the pictures back in Little Penhallow!

After a quick stop for a drink of water, they carried on staunchly up the mountain, passing wind-worn rock faces, trickling streams and tussocks of wildflowers.

'So you're competing in the ice cream competition, I hear?' said Herr Larsen, leading the way.

'Yes, and we're going to win!' Dotty replied confidently. 'Our ice cream is the creamiest, most delicious in the entire world. And that's a fact!'

'I like your confidence, girl,' Herr Larsen replied with a wry smile. 'But you have some stiff competition. I have the Italian competitors staying in one of my outbuildings up at the farm, and they seem very determined.'

'Ha! They have *no* chance,' continued Dotty, seemingly unfazed.

Herr Larsen ruffled her hair with a chuckle. 'And what flavour ice cream are you going to be presenting to the judges?'

'Jam roly-poly pudding,' said Dotty proudly.

Herr Larsen nodded, but was obviously confused. 'Lamb Poly-Moly? I have no idea what that is, but it sounds interesting!'

'*Jam roly-poly!*' corrected Pem with a warm smile. 'It's a traditional British dessert.'

'*Fantastisk!*' said Herr Larsen. 'I'll look forward to trying some. Now come on, not far to go.'

By the time their path finally opened up on to a vast pasture at the very top of the mountain, Orinthia's every breath was a gasp. She stopped for a moment, and looked around, letting her shoulders soften. The sun was casting the mountains in a warm orange light, and there, in front of them, was a small wooden cabin with a pointed rooftop. It looked ever so cosy – clad in red-painted spruce slats with a stout chimney puffing out smoke. The decked porch was adorned with wagon wheels, horseshoes and milk churns – it looked like something you'd find printed on the front of a postcard.

'Welcome to Solskinn Seter!' said Herr Larsen, taking them up to the cabin. '*Seter* is Norwegian for mountain farm.'

He pushed open the front door, causing its glass pane to rattle. The homestead was humble yet welcoming, consisting of a single low rectangular room with timber beams. The stone floor was hard, but the wool curtains at the windows and the woven rugs made the place all the cheerier. Animal hides adorned the walls, alongside a yellowing map of Scandinavia, some framed old photographs hanging slightly askew and a pair of ancient wooden skis.

There was also a small adjoining kitchen with a wood-fired stove, and as Pem and the girls put down their suitcases, Herr Larsen walked over to it and began to stir the contents of a large copper pot on top. The smell coming from it was sweet and comforting, and Orinthia's tummy began to rumble. Thinking about it, she hadn't really eaten much at breakfast, and the walk up the mountain had been rather tiring.

'You can put your ice cream in there,' said Herr Larsen, pointing to the ancient-looking freezer in the corner, its hinges thick with rust. 'And I'll fix us some *rømmegrøt.*' He went to the pot on the stove and added a pinch of something. 'Freshly made today.'

'What's *runnygrooot*?' asked Dotty, her brow furrowing.

Herr Larsen tittered. '*Rømmegrøt* is a bit like porridge. But in Norway we make it with soured cream.'

'Urghhh!' Dotty exclaimed, her nose wrinkling.

'Dotty, don't be so rude!' Pem cut in, giving her daughter a stern look. 'We're in someone else's house.' She turned to Herr Larsen, her cheeks reddening with embarrassment. 'I'm so sorry. She's used to just having boring old ham sandwiches for lunch at home.'

'Aw, don't worry,' the Norwegian man replied, pinching Dotty's cheek playfully. 'Perhaps if I'd mentioned before that we serve *rømmegrøt* with plenty of brown sugar and cinnamon, she might have been more enthusiastic, hmm?'

On hearing the word *sugar*, Dotty's eyes suddenly lit up and she nodded eagerly.

'Excellent,' said Herr Larsen. 'I've laid a table out back. It's such a lovely afternoon. We can eat in the sunshine and wait for your cows to arrive. The Italian guests should already be waiting for us.'

He ushered his new arrivals to the pasture behind the *seter*, where a long wooden table – practically groaning under the delicious-looking spread that he'd prepared – was waiting in the shade of a spruce tree. A dark-haired woman was sitting at its head, her cheeks red with rouge and her eyes obscured by a pair of large tortoiseshell sunglasses. As Orinthia, Dotty and Pem approached, she got up.

'Ah, you must be the Brits?' she exclaimed with an accent not too dissimilar to Mrs Gastaldini's. 'I'm Antonella Dolce. It's very nice to meet you all.'

'Nice to meet you too,' said Pem, extending a hand and making her introductions.

Orinthia and Dotty nodded politely, although Orinthia couldn't help but feel a little pang of animosity towards the Italian woman – she was their rival after all.

A sudden *vroom-vroom* sound came from beneath the table and Antonella tutted. 'Bruno . . . Bruno . . .' she said, lifting up the tablecloth and peering beneath it. 'Come out here and say hello to our new friends, please.'

A scruffy-haired boy, no older than seven, popped out from beneath the table clutching a bright red toy car. He gave Orinthia and Dotty a shy wave, before proceeding to *vroom-vroom* the car up the table leg and into one of the lunch bowls.

'Sorry,' said Antonella, rolling her eyes. 'He's going through a racing driver phase at the moment!'

'It's OK,' Orinthia chuckled, suddenly feeling a lot warmer towards the Italian woman. 'I have a little brother myself, I know what they're like!'

When everyone was settled around the table, Herr Larsen took his guests through every dish on offer, announcing their names in Norwegian before giving an explanation of what they were. There was a platter of preserved codfish known as *tørrfisk*, and a traditional mutton stew called *fårikål*. Cold cuts of meat were accompanied by cloudberry and lingonberry jams, and boiled potatoes were vibrant with fresh dill. Orinthia wasn't entirely convinced by the vinegary pickled herring that Herr Larsen urged her to try, but swallowed it down without fuss nonetheless – their host had gone to so much trouble, after all.

'Whereabouts in Italy are you from, Antonella?' asked Pem, reaching for a piece of bread to dip in her stew.

'We're from . . . Tuscany,' was the reply. 'On the coast.'

'How lovely,' said Orinthia. 'We actually have a

family friend who comes from Naples. Mrs Gastal-dini. She never stops going on about the place. *And* the ice cream.'

Antonella's posture seemed to become more rigid for a moment and she let out a loud cough. 'Well, us Italians are very proud people, that's for sure. Especially when it comes to *gelato*!'

'Let's put our competitiveness aside for the time being and just enjoy this lovely afternoon together,' said Pem with a wry smile. She picked up her glass of wine and tapped Antonella's with a *clink*. 'Cheers! To new friends!'

The sudden beeping of a horn caused everyone around the table to jump.

'Ah! I think this might be your cows, Pem,' said Herr Larsen, pointing across the pasture. An open-top cattle wagon was trundling towards them, and as Orinthia spotted the two pairs of horns and two sets of large ears poking up from the back, she felt her pulse quicken. Fosse and Falaise had arrived at last!

She and Dotty sprinted towards them, and as the wagon pulled up beneath a large spruce tree, Orinthia could already hear the comforting sound of their *moo*s. As Herr Larsen pulled down the rear hatch, the cows lolloped out, and the two girls were by their side in moments. It was so good to see them again, and Orinthia wrapped her arms around Fosse's neck, resting her head on her shoulder. She could feel the cow was shaking slightly, but on the whole seemed well. Falaise leant into Dotty, nuzzling her nose into the crook of the girl's arm, sending her into a ticklish fit of giggles.

'You certainly have those cows well trained,' said Herr Larsen. 'I've never seen a pair come off the wagon so calmly. What's your secret?'

Dotty and Orinthia looked at each other before shimmering their hands with fingers splayed. '*Jaaaaazz!*'

Obviously baffled, Herr Larsen made his way to the wagon's front cab to greet his farmhand. Wanting to say a big thank you themselves, the two girls followed.

But what they saw next stopped them in their tracks. Orinthia felt goosebumps tightening her skin, and her knees buckled.

Sitting in the passenger seat was Monsieur Dubois.

24

'Girls, how nice to see you again,' said Monsieur Dubois, leaning towards the open window and dipping his head in greeting. 'What a coincidence that you are both here.'

Orinthia and Dotty looked at each other and gulped, not knowing what to say. A coincidence? Orinthia certainly didn't think so! But how had Monsieur Dubois found his way here to the *seter*? How had he managed to get a ride in the wagon with Herr Larsen's farmhand?

Orinthia had so many questions, but she knew she

couldn't let her reaction give the game away – she couldn't alert Monsieur Dubois to the fact that she and Dotty knew who he *really* was.

'N-Nice to see you too,' Dotty stammered, obviously trying to pull her mouth into a smile, but looking completely terrified. 'What are you doing here?'

Monsieur Dubois straightened his hat. 'Well, after that dreadful business with Captain Binnacle and my passport I was late disembarking from the *Mollusca* and missed my car. But by a stroke of luck, this kind fellow offered to give me a lift to my guesthouse in his wagon.' He nodded to the man sitting adjacent to him in the cab. 'In fact, would you like me to help you take the cows to one of the barns? It's the least I can—'

'NO!' Orinthia cut in abruptly, not wanting Monsieur Dubois hanging around for a moment longer. Because it wasn't just *their* competition success that was at stake now – if he spotted Antonella and Bruno, he might want to sabotage their chances of winning at the Golden Udder Awards too.

'I mean . . . you've had such a long journey already,' Orinthia backtracked. 'We can take care of the animals from here, Monsieur Dubois.' She couldn't help but say his name with venom, the words feeling like poison on her tongue.

'Yes, we'll be fine from here,' concurred Herr Larsen, much to the girls' relief. 'The cows will probably be happy roaming around the pasture for a while anyway.'

Monsieur Dubois nodded. 'Very well. I guess I'll see you girls at the Golden Udder Awards, if not before.'

The wagon drove off the way it had come, Monsieur Dubois' final words sounding like alarm bells in Orinthia's ears. They had definitely sounded like a threat to her. They'd have to keep their wits about them from now on, and as Herr Larsen made his way back to the lunch table, she hung back to talk to Dotty in private.

'Rinthi, this is awful,' said Dotty, her chin trembling. 'Monsieur Dubois knows where we're staying . . . and . . . and . . . what if he comes back? What if he kidnaps Mam? Or poisons our ice cream? Or—'

'Dotty, breathe,' said Orinthia, putting her hands on her friend's shoulders, trying to calm her. Even though she was terrified herself, Orinthia let her breath out in a slow, steady stream. Panicking was not going to do the situation any good. 'I'm sure we'll be safe here with Herr Larsen. We'll stay in the *seter* all day tomorrow and make sure that your mam doesn't leave either.'

'But how? Mam wants to go sightseeing.'

Orinthia thought for a moment. 'I know! We'll pretend we're ill! We can fake our temperatures and start scratching. Hopefully your mam will think we've caught Taber's chickenpox. And then, on the morning of the competition, we'll have made a miraculous recovery.'

Dotty nodded but looked slightly unsure, before a shout from the lunch table made her flinch.

'Girls, we're going back into the farmhouse for some more *rømmegrøt*!' Pem called out. 'You can leave the cows to graze for a while, then Herr Larsen will take them to the barn before bed.'

'Coming Mam!' Dotty replied, before turning to Orinthia. 'So shall we start pretending that we're ill now?'

'Maybe *after* we've had some more of the *rømmegrøt*,' said Orinthia mischievously. 'I don't want to miss out!'

Back in the *seter* the fireplace had been lit, filling the living room with a sweet-smelling fug. Antonella and Bruno were sitting on one sofa with Pem, and once they'd taken off their shoes, Dotty and Orinthia sank into another. Herr Larsen began dishing up bowls of the Norwegian porridge, and it was just as delicious as he'd promised – luxurious and sweet, with a slight sharpness from the sour cream.

Orinthia was tempted to ask for seconds, but with evening fast approaching, she knew it was time for her and Dotty to start feigning illness. So with Kipling's theatrical ways in the forefront of her mind, she flopped her head down on to one of the cushions, flinging the back of her hand to her forehead. 'Urghhhh,' she groaned. 'Urghhhhhhhhhh.'

'Everything OK, Rinthi?' asked Pem.

'Just feeling a bit hot, that's all,' Orinthia replied meekly, before nodding to Dotty to take the reins.

'Erm . . . come to think of it, I feel a bit sweaty too,' said Dotty, beginning to fan herself.

'Oh dear. Maybe the fire wasn't needed after all,' said Herr Larsen, fetching a pail of water from the sink, and promptly extinguishing the flames with a sizzling hiss. 'There, is that better? The room will cool down soon enough.'

'I-I actually feel a bit itchy,' said Orinthia, continuing with her charade. She began to scratch at her arms and legs, giving Dotty another wink to follow suit.

'My head is itchy too! Ouch! It's horrible!' Dotty said, digging her fingers into her scalp, and raking them through her hair like a monkey with fleas.

Pem's face whitened. 'Oh no! You don't think you've both picked up Taber's chickenpox, do you?'

Orinthia let out a pretend groan. '*Urghhh*, I hope not. That would mean we'd have to stay indoors until we've fully recovered. Dr Badeel said to my mum that chickenpox is highly contagious.'

Dread flashed across poor Pem's face and she turned to the other adults, her cheeks flushing with embarrassment. 'I'm ever so sorry about this, Axel, Antonella. Orinthia's little brother was recovering from chickenpox when we left England.'

'Poor things,' said Herr Larsen. 'The girls do look a little peaky. Why don't you take them up to their room in the attic and I'll prepare some herbal tea, hmm?'

'And don't worry about me and Bruno,' said Antonella. 'Us Italians are made of strong stuff. We have the Mediterranean blood running through our veins after all!'

Obviously completely panicked by the thought that she'd allowed a highly contagious virus to be brought into the *seter*, Pem ignored Antonella's lighthearted comment and quickly ushered the two girls upstairs.

In the attic, two little wooden beds were awaiting Orinthia and Dotty – sleigh-like in shape and made up with thick woollen blankets. There was a larger one for Pem, covered with a shaggy shearling throw.

'I'm so sorry, Pem,' said Orinthia as she opened her suitcase and pulled on her pyjamas. 'This is all *my* fault.'

'Don't be silly, Orinthia,' reassured Pem, but looking more than a little worried as she crossed the room to draw the curtains. 'You were fine when we left Little Penhallow. This can't be helped.'

As she turned on the little nightlight on the dresser, the two girls got into their beds and snuggled down. The hay-stuffed mattress and lambswool blanket were a little musty-smelling but not entirely unpleasant. In fact, Orinthia found the aroma to be quite comforting – as if she were nesting down in a lovely warm barn.

'Right, get some rest,' said Pem, blowing them both kisses. 'I'll be up in a while to see how you're feeling. Shout if you need anything, OK?'

She retreated from the attic, closing the door with a creak. Orinthia and Dotty listened to her footsteps on the stairs, and when they were certain she was out of hearing range, the girls turned to each other.

'I feel so guilty,' whispered Dotty. 'Mam looked so worried.'

'I know,' said Orinthia, equally as remorseful, but confident that they'd done the right thing. 'But we'll be safe here in the *seter* tomorrow and we can spend all day keeping watch.'

'I really hope so,' said Dotty. And letting out a long yawn, she pulled up her covers and was soon snoring peacefully.

Orinthia initially thought that she might write a little in her diary before sleeping. But it wasn't long before her eyes started to droop, and within minutes she'd drifted off too, safe in the knowledge that their plan had worked.

25

Orinthia jolted up in bed, suddenly awake.

A noise was coming from somewhere downstairs, a rittling-rattling sound so loud that it had pulled her from her sleep. Was it Herr Larsen going out to milk the cows? He did say that he got up very early, but surely it was still the middle of the night? She quickly looked at her wristwatch. Yes, it was only half past two!

She cowered in the darkness, listening with increasing trepidation as the rattling continued. A stay in a farmhouse in the middle of the Norwegian mountains would inevitably offer up some unfamiliar sounds, but this wasn't the din of livestock or the whistling of wind through pine trees or the trickling of the fjords. This sounded like . . . someone trying to break in!

Immediately, Orinthia's mind was commandeered by visions of Monsieur Dubois. Had he returned to the *seter*? Was he planning on doing what Dotty had feared – sabotaging their ice cream, or kidnapping Pem, or worse . . . ? With adrenalin shooting through her, Orinthia pushed back her covers and quickly rubbed her face awake. Dotty and Pem were still fast asleep, snoring gently with their knees drawn tightly to their chests. Not wanting to rouse them, Orinthia got out of bed as quietly as she could, and having picked up her torch, she tiptoed to the attic door.

Dotty stirred. 'Rinthi?' she groaned, rubbing her eyes. 'Is it breakfast time? I want some more *runnygrooot*.'

'No, it's not breakfast time yet, Dot,' she whispered. 'Go back to sleep.'

'But where are you going?'

'I-I just need a wee,' she lied, not wanting to worry her friend unnecessarily. 'I'll be back in a minute.'

Dotty nodded sleepily, and rolled back over with a drawn-out yawn.

Having closed the attic door behind her, Orinthia stood at the top of the wooden staircase, listening. There was *definitely* someone moving around downstairs. She could hear footsteps padding around and the sound of heavy breathing. What should she do? Go and investigate? Or run back to the attic and push a chair against the door to keep Pem and Dotty safe?

A sudden crashing sound cut through her thoughts, as something fell to the ground downstairs. There was an angry yelp and Orinthia knew she couldn't stand there any longer. 'Hello?' she called out, clinging cautiously to the bannister as she descended the stairs. The pale moonlight streaming in through a gap in the living-room curtains suddenly dipped as someone passed by. 'Herr Larsen, is that you? Are you OK?'

'Stay where you are!' came a muffled reply. 'I'm armed!'

Orinthia had always thought that if she found herself in such a dangerous predicament, she'd freeze rigid. But she didn't – Herr Larsen had welcomed her into his home and she *had* to protect it.

She brandished her torch and clicked it on, sending a beam of light through the spindles of the bannister. It illuminated a hooded figure standing in the middle of the living room, looking around frantically. She couldn't see their face as it was covered by some kind of balaclava, but they were clutching the tub of jam roly-poly ice cream Pem had brought from home!

Orinthia opened her mouth to shout, but the figure had already pelted across the living room, knocking the torch out of her hand before disappearing out of the front door. The force of the blow sent Orinthia flying backwards, and a sharp pain shot through the back of her head as it met with the end of the bannister.

Dazed, she looked up, but it was too late. The figure was already halfway across the pasture, disappearing into the shadowy protection of the surrounding mountains.

'NO!' Orinthia shouted, slumping to the floor. 'NO, NO, NO!'

'Hey, what's going on out here?'

Orinthia turned to find a bleary-eyed Herr Larsen staggering through the kitchen in his nightshirt and bed socks with an oil lamp in hand.

'Herr Larsen, someone's broken into the farmhouse!' Orinthia cried. She nodded to the ruptured lock of the front door. Herr Larsen let out a loud gasp.

'Oh my goodness!'

'I caught them in the act,' said Orinthia, her body now starting to tremble with shock. 'B-but they got away. I-I c-c-couldn't stop them.' She burst into tears, her face falling into her hands.

'*Herregud!*' Herr Larsen cried, surveying the scene in horror. 'Oh my goodness, an intruder! Orinthia, did you catch sight of them?'

Orinthia looked up, knowing that she couldn't keep her suspicions about Monsieur Dubois a secret any longer. 'I didn't see their face, but I think I know who it was. That man in the front of the wagon yesterday, Dotty and I met him on board the *Mollusca*. We think he's been trying to sabotage our chances of winning the Golden Udder Awards and . . .' Her words had been coming thick and fast and she paused for breath. 'And that's why he broke in! He came to steal our ice creams! I saw him with a tub!'

'WHAT?' came a stern voice from the top of the stairs. Pem was there with Dotty and she'd obviously been listening to everything that had just been divulged. 'Are you sure about this, Orinthia?'

Orinthia nodded. 'His handwriting matched the horrible note that was left in the *Penny Lick*, and he knew about Fosse and Falaise and—'

Pem pelted down the stairs and pulled Orinthia to her in a tight squeeze. She was trembling. 'Why on earth didn't either of you talk to me about this?'

'We didn't want to worry you, Mam,' Dotty replied, slinking meekly down the stairs towards them. 'We thought we could deal with him by ourselves.'

'Oh my goodness, Dotty Ambrose!' she scolded, trembling with rage and worry. 'You should never, ever keep anything like that from me. What were you thinking?'

'I kept it from you too,' said Orinthia, looking up. 'This isn't just on Dotty.'

Pem breathed out sharply. 'Don't you worry, young lady, I know that. But are you OK? Did this man hurt you at all?'

Orinthia shook her head, even though it was pounding terribly. 'I just fell as he ran out the door.'

'Well let's get you on to the sofa immediately. Dotty, run upstairs and get some blankets. Axel, maybe you could make Orinthia something sweet for the shock?'

'Of-of course,' stuttered Herr Larsen, looking as though he could desperately do with some sugar himself. 'And don't worry, everything's going to be fine. I'm going to call the police immediately. Chief Pedersen is extremely good at his job and hopefully this man won't have got too far.'

'Thank you,' Pem replied. 'And in the meantime, I'll go and check that Antonella and Bruno are OK. Hopefully Monsieur Dubois didn't find his way into their barn—'

On hearing the word *barn*, Orinthia jumped up. 'Fosse and Falaise!' she shouted, her heart suddenly in her throat. 'We have to check that they're OK!'

Not waiting to see if anyone from the *seter* was following, Orinthia dashed into the night. It was cold now, a biting wind pushing against her despite the protection of the mountains. The wiry grasses of the pasture scratched against her bare feet as she ran towards the barn, not looking back for a moment. Why hadn't she thought of checking on the cows earlier? They'd be an obvious target for Monsieur Dubois!

Orinthia came to a skidding halt, gasping.

The barn door was wide open, its lock bust like the farmhouse's.

Orinthia edged inside, almost deafened by the complete absence of sound. There was no tinkling of cowbells. No lowing. No rustling of straw beneath hoof.

'Fosse?' she called out through the darkness. 'Falaise?'

There was no *mooo* in reply.

And to her horror, the stall that Fosse and Falaise had bedded down in the previous evening was empty.

26

By the time the police had been called, everyone, including Antonella and Bruno, had congregated in the living room, and were snuggled up under woollen blankets. Having checked the freezer Pem confirmed that their jam roly-poly ice cream had been pilfered by Monsieur Dubois. Dotty sat sobbing uncontrollably, her eyes red and her cheeks flushed.

Herr Larsen, who had rekindled the fire, was passing round a plate of butter cookies to go with a pot of tea. But the sweet treats did little to settle Orinthia's nerves. The shock of what had just happened had left her insides churning. What she'd done had been reckless, impulsive – thank goodness Monsieur Dubois had fled when he did, rather than kidnapping her too!

The Italians had been lucky – Monsieur Dubois hadn't gone anywhere near their barn, and their ice cream ingredients hadn't been touched. But Antonella was clearly shaken. 'I can't believe this has happened,' she kept repeating, holding her son close. 'It's awful. Just awful!'

There was a knock at the broken front door, and a man, presumably Chief Pedersen, poked his head around it. He was burly, dressed in uniform and a peaked cap with gold insignia.

'Good evening, Chief Pedersen,' said Herr Larsen, getting to his feet. 'Thank you for coming so quickly. Please come in.'

The policeman sat down on the sofa next to Pem, and as Herr Larsen explained what had happened, he began to jot some notes, his pen scritch-scratching against the paper as he took down the details.

'This is highly unprecedented,' said Chief Pedersen once Herr Larsen had finished. He surveyed the scene, his brow furrowing. 'Orinthia, Herr Larsen said that you were awoken by unusual sounds, so you came downstairs and found someone in the living room? Is that correct?'

Orinthia nodded and Pem reached for her hand. 'Yes. I heard the front door rattling, then there was a crash. I came downstairs and found Monsieur Dubois. He knocked me over then ran away.'

As she talked, Chief Pedersen continued to scribble in his notebook. 'And you're *sure* it was this Dubois character?' he asked. 'It couldn't have been someone lost on the mountain? A trekker looking for shelter having taken a wrong path?'

'No!' Orintha replied sharply. 'I know it was him! Who else would have reason to steal our cows and our ice cream?'

'And a trekker wouldn't have fled so quickly if interrupted, would they?' said Herr Larsen, much to Orinthia's relief.

'Erm . . . yes . . . good point,' said the police chief, obviously a little embarrassed. 'It's just so unusual. We don't usually see crime up here in the mountains.'

'I know,' said Herr Larsen, examining the lock once more and shaking his head in disbelief. 'Solskinn Seter has been in my family for hundreds of years and not once has it been broken into.'

Chief Pedersen thought for a moment, running a hand through his beard. 'Well, what I'm going to do is get a couple of my men to search the area. Most likely, the intruder is hiding out with the cows in the mountains somewhere.'

'Poor Fosse, poor Falaise,' yelped Dotty. 'They're going to be so scared.'

'Don't worry,' Chief Pedersen replied. 'I have a very good team. We'll find your cows.' He turned to Herr Larsen. 'But I'd probably secure your front door with something temporarily, Axel. Just to be on the safe side.'

Herr Larsen nodded. 'I will. And I'll sleep in the living room to keep watch.'

'What?' Orinthia exclaimed. 'We can't just go back to sleep! We all need to be out there looking for Fosse and Falaise too. The more people searching, the better—'

'Orinthia, it's the middle of the night,' said Pem, putting a hand on her shoulder. 'What use are we going to be? Chief Pedersen's men are the best people for the job. The police know what they're doing, we can trust them—'

'Oh yes, just like we could trust DI Snodgrass!' Orinthia snapped sarcastically. 'What an honourable policeman *he* turned out to be!'

Chief Pedersen looked confused. 'I don't know who this DI Snodgrass is, Orinthia, but I can assure you that *my* officers are extremely dependable. They know these mountains better than anyone.'

'And besides, you girls can't be running around in the cold with your fevers,' said Pem. 'You need to rest.'

Orinthia and Dotty looked at each other, unable to hide the guilt on their faces.

Clocking that she'd been lied to, Pem sighed heavily. 'You're not ill at all, are you? You pretended?'

Dotty's eyes filled with tears. 'Only because we didn't want you to take us sightseeing tomorrow. We were so scared that Monsieur Dubois might kidnap us that we didn't want to leave the *seter*.'

Pem ran her hands through her hair. 'Oh you silly, silly girls. If only you'd told me about Monsieur Dubois and your suspicions when we were on the ship. We could have contacted the police immediately and all of this could have been avoided.'

Orinthia looked to her feet. Pem was right. Once again, she'd put herself and others in danger. Mum was going to be so angry, so disappointed. She looked to the window, not knowing what to do or say.

'Mam, what are we going to do about the Golden Udder Awards?' asked Dotty from beneath her blankets. 'Even if we get Fosse and Falaise back, we don't have our ice cream.'

'You, Orinthia and your mother could use my kitchen to make a new batch?' suggested Herr Larsen. 'We have plenty of ingredients here you could use? Berries, fruits, herbs, sugar, cream. You might be able to make an even better version of your . . . what did you call it again . . . jam roly-poly?'

Dotty shook her head. 'It won't be the same. We made the strawberry sauce using my mum's home-made jam and it'll be impossible to replicate. The recipe's been in her family for decades and it's top secret.'

Orinthia thought for a moment. 'Well, how about if we telephone Grandy Brock and ask if one of the animails could deliver a sample of the ice cream to us in Norway? You have some left over in the creamery, right?'

Dotty's eyes lit up at the suggestion. 'Yes! Can we, Mam? Please?'

Pem sat back. 'I don't see why not. But only if it's not too much trouble for Grandy Brock. I know how busy he is at the menagerie at the moment.'

'He won't mind!' Orinthia replied, sitting up straight. 'He'd do anything to help out, I know it. We can ask him to send Helios, our golden eagle, with a cool bag.'

Dotty nodded eagerly. 'So you'll call him in the morning, Mam? You promise?'

Pem nodded, obviously tired. 'Yes, I promise.'

Antonella's eyes had widened in shock. 'But surely this bird won't make it here in time for the Golden Udder Awards? They can't fly *that* fast, surely?'

'Golden eagles can fly at speeds of nearly a hundred and thirty kilometres per hour!' Orinthia replied proudly, pushing her shoulders back. 'If Helios leaves Little Penhallow tomorrow morning he'll be with us in seven hours. Eight max!'

Antonella spluttered in disbelief. 'Well . . . that's wonderful news. I'm so . . . pleased . . . for you.'

Once Chief Pedersen had taken a few more notes, he left the *seter* to round up his troops.

'Right, I think we should all try and get some sleep,' said Pem, clapping her hands together. She got up and gestured for the girls to follow. Even though Orinthia would have preferred to put on her coat and boots and join the police with their search, she knew it was best to do as Dotty's mam said.

But up in the attic, despite being hunkered down under her mound of snuggly blankets, Orinthia couldn't drop off. No matter how tight she closed her eyes she just couldn't fall asleep. The rest of the night was torturous. She couldn't decide what was more devastating – the fact that she and Dotty had let Pem down so badly, or the fact that Fosse and Falaise were out in the wilds of Norway all alone. Orinthia couldn't help thinking back to the day when Geronimo went missing. She remembered how Taber's face had crumpled as Grandy Brock reluctantly admitted that they might never see their beloved pelican again.

Of course, that story had ended happily, but what if this one didn't?

27

The next morning, Orinthia, Dotty and Pem awoke to find Herr Larsen standing on the threshold of the attic room. His boots were muddy and his brow sweaty. He'd obviously been out on the mountain and Orinthia prayed that he was bringing good news about the cows.

'Have they been found?' Orinthia blurted out, flinging back her blankets. 'Are Fosse and Falaise back?'

'I'm so sorry, Orinthia, but it is not good news,' said Herr Larsen, shaking his head gravely. 'The police were out all night but there have been no sightings. I went out searching this morning as well, but to no avail, I'm afraid.'

Orinthia crumpled, disappointment and anger and sadness rising up inside her all at once. 'Well, you obviously weren't searching hard enough!' she blurted out. She knew she should shut up, but she couldn't control what was coming out of her mouth. 'I knew we should have gone out looking ourselves. I bet you were hoping we'd fail in the competition all along, so that Norway had a better chance at winning!'

Herr Larsen's brow darkened and Orinthia knew immediately that what she'd just said was completely unacceptable. She quickly opened her mouth to apologize but he was already walking towards her. 'I'll have you know that I was up at dawn taping these posters to every tree in Bergen!' he said, reaching into his bag and pulling out a sheet of paper. He threw it on to the table beside Orinthia's bed, making her flinch. On it there was a black-and-white photo of Fosse and Falaise followed by some Norwegian and an English translation:

MISSING ANIMALS

TWO GUERNSEY COWS

ANSWERING TO THE NAMES FOSSE AND FALAISE.
LAST SEEN AT SOLSKINN SETER.
IF ANYONE HAS ANY INFORMATION,
PLEASE CONTACT CHIEF PEDERSEN AT
BERGEN POLICE STATION.

Orinthia didn't know what to say. Her tummy was churning with guilt. 'I'm-I'm so sorry, Herr Larsen. I'm just so upset. I wasn't thinking straight and—'

'You can say that again,' Herr Larsen said sadly. He looked so offended, so disappointed, and Orinthia could feel her chin beginning to wobble.

'Axel, what Orinthia said was wrong, but she's just a child,' said Pem, edging forward and trying to appease Herr Larsen. 'She made a mistake and she's apologized . . .'

Herr Larsen shook his head, tutting loudly. 'I appreciate that, but our community is built on trust and cooperation. Not accusation and condemnation. I was more than happy to help in their search for the cows, but this kind of behaviour is not acceptable.'

He turned on his heel and left the attic in silence, leaving Orinthia in tears.

'What did you go and do that for?' Dotty snapped.

'I know you're worried, but there was no need for you to be so rude!'

Orinthia sniffed back her sobs. She'd never seen Dotty angry before and her words really stung. 'Sorry for *actually* caring about what's happened to our cows!' she retorted, taken aback by her friend's tone.

'I *do* care!' Dotty countered. 'But without Herr Larsen's help we're never going to find Fosse and Falaise. You were so bad-mannered back then that he's probably on his way to tell the police to call off the search—'

Pem sprang from her bed, leaping between the two girls. 'That's enough!' she scolded, holding up her hands to quell the squabble. 'I can't believe that after everything that's happened, you two think it's a good idea to start fighting.'

She turned to her daughter and glared. 'Dotty, Orinthia's behaviour was unacceptable but she knows that, so I don't want to hear another word from you, OK?'

She looked to Orinthia. 'Rinthi, I'd like you to go and apologize to Herr Larsen at once. Our Norwegian host has been nothing but kind to us, and I don't want him to think that we don't appreciate everything that he's done. What you said before was extremely out of character and I'm sure your mother would not be impressed.'

Orinthia nodded meekly and, dropping her chin to her chest, she slunk downstairs.

28

Herr Larsen accepted Orinthia's apology but kept out of her way for the remainder of the morning. She really hoped he knew how truly sorry she was. She'd never spoken to a grown-up in such a way, let alone a grown-up who'd welcomed her into his home, and had been so kind and helpful and warm. She decided that once she'd returned to Little Penhallow she'd write to him to apologize once again, and maybe buy him a present with her pocket money. She wondered if he'd appreciate some bonbons from Mr Barnabas's sweet shop.

Things with Dotty, however, remained tense. Pem had spoken to Grandy Brock after breakfast, and even though he'd agreed to send Helios with the ice cream straight away, Dotty had refused to engage with any of Orinthia's excitement. 'Isn't it great news, Dot?' Orinthia had exclaimed, to which Dotty had shrugged before walking off into another room.

After lunch, Pem had suggested that she take the two girls down to the quayside for a trip on the funicular, as Herr Larsen had said it would be closing that evening for maintenance. Orinthia thought it was probably a good idea – it might take their minds off things for a little while at least. She glanced across the room to gauge Dotty's reaction, but the girl immediately looked away. She obviously still hadn't forgiven Orinthia and was making no attempt to hide the fact. 'I'm not going if *she's* going,' Dotty said pointedly, crossing her arms across her chest.

Pem tutted loudly. 'Fine. Orinthia and I shall go out and you can stay here.'

Dotty frowned. 'What? That's so unfair! *She's* the one who was rude this morning. Why should I be punished?'

'Dotty Ambrose, that's quite enough!' snapped Pem, her brow darkening. 'What did I say about—'

'It's OK, Pem,' Orinthia cut in, not wanting to cause any more animosity. 'Dotty can go with you to the funicular. I'll just stay here and wait for Helios. It will be good for him to see a familiar face when he arrives with the ice cream.'

Pem huffed. 'Well, only if you're sure?'

Orinthia nodded, trying to hide her sadness.

'OK, but under no circumstances are you to leave the *seter*. No wandering off to look for Fosse and Falaise, you promise me?'

Orinthia nodded once more, although it was going to be a hard promise to keep – she was still eager to go and join the police in their search for the missing cows.

As Pem and Dotty made their way across the pasture towards the mountain track, Orinthia sat watching at the window. Her tummy was in knots and she could feel tears welling in her eyes once more – she'd already managed to upset her new best friend and they'd only known each other a short while! What a disaster this trip to Norway had turned out to be. The only comfort was the fact that Helios would be here soon enough with the ice cream. Maybe he'd even bring a letter from Grandy Brock and the gang? Or something from Mum?

After a while, Orinthia wandered into the kitchen, hoping that there might be some *rømmegrøt* left over from breakfast to have as a little snack. She was greeted by Antonella, who was slicing a loaf of rye bread atop one of the wooden counters. Little Bruno was sitting at the table holding out an empty plate impatiently.

'*Ciao*, Orinthia! I am just making some sandwiches,' said Antonella. 'Would you like one too? I am doing cheese and tomato. *Formaggio e pomodoro!*'

On hearing the word *pomodoro*, Orinthia's thoughts immediately turned to Mrs Gastaldini, and a sudden pang of homesickness coursed through her body. How she missed being at Tupenny Mill with her friends and brothers. She wished she'd never come to Norway in the first place. She nodded wistfully and sat down at the table with Bruno. 'Thank you, Antonella, that would be lovely.'

'But why are you on your own? Where are Dotty and Pem today?'

'They're on the funicular. It closes this evening for maintenance so they wanted to take a ride before we go home.'

A strange expression of alertness suddenly passed over Antonella's face, as if she'd just had an epiphany.

'The funicular closes this evening, you say?'

Orinthia nodded. 'Yes, Herr Larsen said they shut it for a couple of days once a month to check that everything is in order.'

For a moment, Antonella stood deep in thought. It was as if she was in a daydream.

'Everything OK?' Orinthia probed.

Antonella blinked suddenly, snapping from her trance. 'Oh, yes, yes. It's . . . erm . . . just a shame about the funicular, that's all – I would have liked to have taken Bruno. We won't have time, now.' She placed Orinthia's sandwich down on the table and cut it in two with the bread knife. 'Anyway, there you go. Eat.'

Orinthia took a big bite of her sandwich and sat back, enjoying the mouthful. It was nice to be eating something so comforting, so homely, after having to endure so much pickled fish!

'How's your preparation going for the competition anyway?' she asked Antonella.

The Italian woman sat down next to her. '*Bene, bene*. But we're here to enjoy the experience rather than focusing too much on winning,' she said graciously. 'What about your eagle? Is he on his way? What time are you expecting him?'

Orinthia looked to the kitchen clock. 'In the next hour or so. And hopefully the police will find Fosse and Falaise soon too.'

Antonella smiled and patted Orinthia's arm. 'That's great. But don't get your hopes up, hmm? I'd hate for you to be disappointed if things don't work out.'

Orinthia nodded begrudgingly. Why did grown-ups always have to be so pessimistic, so measured? Nothing good ever came from giving up hope. You just had to stay positive.

This, however, was easier said than done. When Pem and Dotty arrived back from the funicular just before dinner, there was still no sign of Helios or the two cows.

The atmosphere over dinner was gloomy. Herr Larsen had put out another abundant spread, but Orinthia didn't feel hungry, and instead was lifting up spoonfuls of soup from her bowl and letting them slop back with a *splosh*. Dotty looked equally as crestfallen, and was staring out of the window, letting her food go cold.

'Bruno and Antonella not joining us tonight?' asked Pem, obviously trying to lighten the mood.

'No, they went out a little while ago,' said Herr Larsen, piling his plate with potato salad and rye bread. 'Said something about eating in town this evening.'

Pem nodded. 'And no news from Chief Pedersen?'

Herr Larsen lowered his head gravely. 'Unfortunately not, I'm afraid.'

'Well, that's that then,' Dotty blurted out, banging her fork on to her plate. 'Helios isn't here with our ice cream and we don't have the cows. We may as well pack our bags and go home now!'

'Don't be silly, Dot,' said Pem, trying to calm her distraught daughter. 'There's still plenty of time for Helios to get here. And if Fosse and Falaise don't turn up, we *can* still compete without them.'

Orinthia nodded. The thought of entering the competition without their beloved cows was horrible, but it would be a shame to have come all the way here and not present to the judges at all.

But Dotty was obviously not convinced. 'What? There's no way I'm going on stage without them. It'll make me feel even worse.'

Pem sighed heavily, obviously at her wits' end. 'Fine. If in the morning there's no sign of Helios or the cows, then we'll just go to the town hall and enjoy the Golden Udder Awards as spectators. Why don't you come with us, Axel?'

'That sounds wonderful,' the Norwegian man replied. 'Count me in.'

'That settles it then,' said Pem, looking to the two girls as if to say the case was closed. 'If we're unable to compete, it will be nice for us to be there to support Antonella and Bruno.'

Orinthia puffed out her cheeks. She couldn't bear the thought of watching the Golden Udder being handed to somebody else. But she'd promised Mum that she wouldn't misbehave, and having failed spectacularly so far, she knew that she couldn't put another foot out of line.

29

If their plans for the competition hadn't gone so horribly wrong, Orinthia would have gasped with delight on entering Bergen Town Hall the following morning. But with still no sign of Helios or the cows, she was feeling more than a little glum.

With Pem, Dotty and Herr Larsen in tow, she reluctantly pushed open the double doors to a grand lobby which was buzzing with excitement. There were swarms of people milling around – supporters, spectators and even some journalists from the local newspaper who'd come to interview the entrants. In the far corner, a man and a woman were standing in front of a large Norwegian flag, surrounded by reporters and cameras. They were obviously the local competitors and were being treated as if they were national heroes.

'So, are you both looking forward to what the day has in store?' asked one of the journalists, holding out a microphone.

'Oh, yes,' replied the Norwegian man, illuminated by the flashbulbs of the cameras. 'We're very excited about bringing our ice cream to the judging table.'

Another reporter chimed in with her notebook and pen poised. 'And are you confident about your chances of winning?'

'Very,' replied the woman with a proud smile. 'The Golden Udder and the cash prize are staying here in Bergen!'

Orinthia felt her heart sink. She, Dotty and Pem should have been doing interviews like this too. *They* should be having their photos taken and enthusing about the incredible delights they'd be serving the judges.

Pem, obviously sensing her sadness, leant in and gave her a big squeeze. 'There's always next year,' she whispered warmly. 'And besides, it's probably fair

226

that we give the other competitors a chance just this once, hmm?'

Orinthia looked up to her and smiled. Pem always managed to put a positive spin on things. But that wasn't going to stop her from keeping an eye out for Helios. There was always a chance that he could still arrive in time for them to compete, and Fosse and Falaise could still be found. With Dotty already looking around the lobby eagle-eyed, she knew that they were on the same page, despite having barely uttered a word to each other in days.

As the crowd began to shift, Pem, Herr Larsen and the two girls made their way into the auditorium. It was equally breathtaking, with seating set across two tiers and a huge stage framed with plush red velvet curtains. To the right-hand side of the stage, a small band consisting of fiddlers, horn players and a percussionist was playing a piece of lively Norwegian folk music.

They settled in their seats, and as the lights dimmed, the audience hushed. A short, bulbous man appeared on stage wearing a heavily embroidered woollen suit which Orinthia could only assume was the traditional dress of Norway. He had the largest moustache that Orinthia had ever seen, so huge that it almost warranted a stage of its own!

'That's Mayor Rasmussen,' Herr Larsen whispered. 'He's going to be hosting the competition.'

The moustachioed man tapped the microphone in front of him, and the audience instantly sat to attention. '*God ettermiddag alle sammen*,' he bellowed. 'Good afternoon, everyone. As Mayor of Bergen it is my pleasure to welcome you all to the inaugural Golden Udder Awards, where we will be celebrating the finest in ice cream making from all over the globe. Who will be the *cream* of the crop this year, I wonder?' He tittered at his own joke and Orinthia cringed. Old men always made such awful wisecracks! They just weren't funny!

The mayor continued, 'To start, I'd like to introduce you to this year's esteemed judge. She is head of Norway's most famous purveyors of frozen desserts, Magisk Iskrem, and holds the world record for most ice cream sundaes eaten in an hour. Please, put your hands together for Ms Perdita Pamplemousse!'

He swept a hand into the air, triggering a huge round of applause. The band began to play once more, filling the auditorium with another jaunty song.

'Perdita Pamplemousse. What a lovely name,' whispered Orinthia to Pem. 'She sounds like an ice cream flavour herself! Something sweet and fruity!'

'Ha! I wouldn't be so sure about that,' said Herr Larsen, shaking his head forlornly. 'She's a bit of a battleaxe, if truth be told. Infamous for her temper here in Norway. She once made our prime minister cry during a television interview!'

As Ms Pamplemousse walked on to the stage, it didn't take long for Herr Larsen's assessment to be confirmed. The woman was a tiny, shrew-like creature, with a scowl on her face and her arms crossed tightly over her chest. For someone who was just about to be given a load of free ice cream to taste, she looked positively gloomy.

'Told you!' said Herr Larsen with a cheeky wink. 'What a grumpy old crone.'

Up on stage, Mayor Rasmussen held out a welcoming arm to the judge. 'So, Perdita, what are you looking for in this year's ice creams?' he asked, as the audience quietened once more.

'What I always look for,' said Perdita, pushing her grey, bobbed hair behind her ears without a hint of a smile. 'Perfection. And nothing less.'

Unclear as to whether this was a joke or not, the audience tittered nervously, but from the look in

Perdita Pamplemousse's beady eyes there was no doubt that she was deadly serious.

'Erm . . . OK,' said Mayor Rasmussen awkwardly. 'But are there any particular flavours you're hoping to sample today?'

'Anything but mint chocolate chip,' was Perdita's surly reply. 'That flavour combination is the devil's work! The devil's work, I tell you!'

Mayor Rasmussen gulped, and just then the sound of someone leaving their seat in a hurry echoed around the auditorium. Orinthia looked up to see one of the competitors snatching up her belongings and fleeing the auditorium in tears.

'Well . . . I think I know what flavour *she* was planning to serve,' said Mayor Rasmussen with a gulp. 'If anyone else was planning on presenting mint choc chip then maybe you should make a quick exit too.'

Perdita Pamplemousse harrumphed. 'Or even better, have your tastebuds transplanted immediately.'

There was more uncomfortable laughter, and Orinthia and Pem shared a troubled look.

'Anyway, moving on . . .' said the mayor, looking down at his clipboard and running a finger along it. 'Before we start, I need to make you aware that unfortunately, due to unforeseen circumstances, the British competitors have decided to withdraw from this year's competition. We wish them all the best, and hope to see them next year.' He raised a hand in their direction, causing Orinthia to sink down into her seat with humiliation. 'Now, without further ado, I would like to invite Ms Pamplemousse to take her seat at the judging table.'

There were cheers from the audience as the judge settled down. She put her handbag on the table and proceeded to take out a large magnifying glass, a spittoon, a notebook and pen, and a delicate silver tasting spoon. She definitely meant business!

'How does the scoring work?' Orinthia whispered to Pem. 'What will Perdita be looking for?'

'She'll be considering taste, texture, appearance and smell. Then she'll give each competitor a final mark out of ten.'

Orinthia nodded, and as Mayor Rasmussen declared the competition officially open, she urged herself to try and enjoy the show.

First to face the judge was the German competitor, Klaus Breckendorf. He appeared on stage dressed in lederhosen, to the sounds of some traditional Bavarian *Volksmusik*. His Black Forest ice cream was a sight to behold – rich in chocolate and decorated with cherries of the deepest purple.

He yodelled as he served his sample, and once he'd stepped back, Perdita Pamplemousse wasted no time in getting down to business. She smelt the ice cream first, putting her nose into the bowl and taking short, sharp sniffs as if she were a bloodhound. Then, picking up her magnifying glass, she began to eyeball the sample intently. Some furious note-taking followed, before she finally took a spoonful of the ice cream to her lips, and sucked it in slowly. Without giving anything away she began to swill and slosh her mouthful from cheek to cheek as if tasting a fine wine, before emptying what was left into her spittoon with a *sploosh*.

Klaus Breckendorf was edging nervously from foot to foot and Orinthia started to think about how she'd be feeling if she were about to go up on stage. Terrified, no doubt, but that didn't stop her from quickly glancing around the auditorium to check if Helios had miraculously found his way to them. To her dismay, he was nowhere to be seen.

'And your score for the German competitor, please, Perdita,' prompted Mayor Rasmussen.

'One out of ten,' said Perdita Pamplemousse, holding up her scoreboard. 'Uneven distribution of cherries, melted too quickly on the tongue, and tasted like old socks.'

The audience gasped with horror and Orinthia looked to Pem in shock. Herr Larsen had warned that Perdita was going be a tough critic, but this feedback was brutal. Even the mayor seemed to be taken aback by her unabashedly negative remarks.

'Erm . . . so that's a grand total of one point for Klaus Breckendorf of Germany!' he said with obvious embarrassment. 'A great start to the competition. Let's give him a round of applause, shall we?'

The audience clapped out of politeness, but unsurprisingly the German competitor looked mortified. He ran off stage, and it was no surprise to anyone to hear his violent sobs emanating from the wings.

For the next hour or so the audience watched from the edge of their seats as, one by one, the other competitors graced the stage. The Swiss contestant Clarissa Fankhauser's offering was an alpine strawberry sorbet which, in Orinthia's opinion, looked deliciously refreshing, but was awarded a measly two points by Perdita Pamplemousse for being 'too cold by far!' The poor competitors from Canada, seemingly confident in presenting their maple syrup knickerbocker glory, were awarded just half a point.

The morning's lowest score, however, was given to Demetri Galanis from Athens for his Greek salad sundae. He'd seemed more than confident in presenting his cucumber-and-tomato ice cream, swirled with feta and topped with an olive, but Perdita Pamplemousse had soon quashed his optimism. 'This ice cream gets ZERO points,' she'd announced. 'And that's me being generous. It's disgusting. I wouldn't feed it to my worst enemy!'

The audience shifted uncomfortably in their seats, whispers of incredulity passing from row to row:

'How can she award anyone a *zero*?'

'She's being so harsh . . .'

'Is *anyone* going to win the Golden Udder Award?'

Herr Larsen turned to Pem. 'Wow. Maybe having your cows stolen was actually a blessing in disguise,' he whispered. 'I'm not sure I would have wanted you to be subjected to Perdita's wrath.'

'But she would have enjoyed *our* entry!' Dotty protested. 'I *know* she would have. I just *know* it!' A tear rolled down her cheek and Orinthia sighed. Dotty was right of course – the jam roly-poly pudding recipe had been so delicious that even a grumpy old witch like Perdita Pamplemousse would have found it impossible to fault.

Orinthia reached over and squeezed her friend's hand. 'Don't worry, there's still time for Helios to get here, Dot. And if not, next year we'll come back bigger and better, I promise. We'll train up every animal in the menagerie to serve ice creams if we have to!'

Dotty looked up and smiled awkwardly. 'Thanks, Rinthi. And I'm sorry that we fell out. It's just that—'

'It's fine,' Orinthia whispered. 'You were right. My behaviour *was* out of order. Friends?'

Dotty sniffed back her tears. 'Yes. Best friends.'

30

At midday, Mayor Rasmussen declared that it was time to break for lunch, and that the competition would resume at one o'clock. Antonella and Bruno's stracciatella ice cream had garnered the highest score of the morning so far, albeit only four points, and despite her own disappointment at not being able to compete, Orinthia was really happy for them. As the house lights went up, the audience gathered their belongings and started to make their way up the gangways to the exits. Everyone looked as though they'd just come off the most tumultuous of rollercoasters – Perdita Pamplemousse had certainly taken them all on a very bumpy ride!

'What a morning!' declared Pem, as she, Orinthia, Dotty and Herr Larsen made their way back through the lobby to get some much-needed fresh air. 'That judge is such a bully! All those poor competitors whose ice cream recipes she tore to shreds.' She shook her head in disgust. 'Anyway, what would you all like for lunch? I thought that maybe we could find Antonella and Bruno then wander down to the quay-side and get some fresh fish?'

'That's a wonderful idea,' Herr Larsen replied. 'I know just the place. They do the best vinegared squid rings in Bergen!'

Orinthia was less than enthused by the idea of eating more pickled seafood, but remembering the hawker she'd spotted selling lingonberry waffles and pancakes on the quayside when they got off the ferry, she was happy to go along with the idea.

But just as they were about to leave, she suddenly noticed that she was missing her camera. 'Drat, I've left it inside,' she said, patting herself down and realizing that it must still be beneath her seat in the auditorium. 'I'll just go and fetch it. You lot go on ahead and I'll catch up with you. I'll see if I can find

Antonella and Bruno, too.'

'I'll come with you,' said Dotty, before turning to her mother. 'I don't want Orinthia walking around by herself.'

'OK,' said Pem. 'But stick together and don't be long. No dilly-dallying.'

The two girls headed back inside, picking their way through the crowd of people still milling around. Orinthia could still hear people talking about the zero score which Perdita Pamplemousse had awarded to the Greek competitor. It was obviously something that would go down in competition history.

As soon as they got back into the auditorium, Orinthia ran back to her seat to get her camera. Having dusted it off, she swung its strap over her shoulder and was just making her way back to the gangway when a whiff of something unpleasant wafted up her nose.

She sniffed, then balked, trying to work out what it was.

'Rinthi, what is it?' asked Dotty, clocking her friend's distracted expression.

'I can smell something weird,' Orinthia whispered, her nose in the air as she tried to locate the source of the pong. It seemed to be emanating from under the next row of seats, and she dropped to her knees in exploration.

'Aha!' she exclaimed, pulling out a pair of old walking boots. They were covered in what appeared to be mud, but as Orinthia brought them closer to her nose, she quickly realized that they were actually caked with . . . cow poo!

Dotty leant forward, and having got a whiff of the crusty brown dung, she snapped back to Orinthia, her eyes wide. 'Hang on, is that—?'

Orinthia nodded, and without needing to say another word, the two girls sprinted back through the auditorium to the lobby, taking the boots with them. Most of the audience had left the building by now, and apart from a couple of ushers standing around, it was pretty much empty. Leaping behind a large potted plant, the friends took a moment to catch their breaths.

'That poo *has* to belong to either Fosse or Falaise!' whispered Dotty, looking around. 'It's just too much of a coincidence. Monsieur Dubois must have come here, before discarding his boots and hiding the cows somewhere in the building. We need to go and look for them!'

Orinthia calmed herself, and catching sight of a

door bearing the words BACKSTAGE ENTRANCE, she gestured towards it. 'Let's try and go through there. There's bound to be loads of secret rooms and corridors behind the stage. Perfect for hiding away a couple of animals!'

Keeping their eyes peeled for busybodies, the two girls pelted towards the backstage door. But much to their frustration, it was locked. Orinthia grabbed hold of a nearby sideboard to anchor herself and began to pull . . .

'Excuse me! Can I help you?' came a sharp voice from behind.

Terrified, the two girls wheeled round to find the rosy-cheeked usher who'd taken their tickets earlier on.

'We need to go backstage,' said Dotty. 'Could you open the door for us, please?'

'That area is for competitors and authorized personnel only,' replied the usher. 'I can't let you through, I'm afraid.'

'We were *meant* to be competing,' said Orinthia. 'But . . . well it's a long story . . . anyway, we left some things in the dressing room. We need to go and get them.'

'Oh, you're the British competitors that pulled out last minute?' said the usher, flashing them a smug smile. 'Probably for the best, seeing that *our* Norwegian team are the favourites to win this year. You didn't want to make fools of yourselves, I understand.'

'That's right,' said Orinthia through gritted teeth, trying to pull her face into an expression that didn't say, *You're talking absolute rubbish! We would have definitely won!*

Dotty, on the other hand, wasn't quite so subtle in her reaction. 'Are you going to let us through or not?' she snapped.

The old woman *ummed* and *ahhhed*, and Orinthia was just about to tell her to forget it when a familiar voice rung through the lobby.

'Orinthia, Dotty? Is everything OK?'

The two girls looked round to find Antonella striding towards them, with Bruno by her side.

'Oh, Antonella, thank goodness you're here!' Dotty exclaimed. 'We think Monsieur Dubois has hidden Fosse and Falaise backstage! Could you tell this woman to let us through, please? We need to go and look for them.'

Antonella seemed startled, and her eyes darted towards the locked backstage door. 'Are you sure? I doubt very much that he would have brought them here today, of all places—'

'Maybe not,' interrupted Orinthia, brandishing the stinky boots. 'But we found these in the auditorium and they're covered in cow dung! So he's *definitely* been here at some point. We need to go backstage see if he left any clues behind.'

Antonella sighed before whispering something to Bruno in Italian and handing him a few coins. He nodded, before skipping across the lobby and out of the front doors.

'These girls are with me,' said Antonella to the usher. 'You can let them through.'

The usher sighed. 'Well, I'm not really meant to—'

'Just do as I say!' snapped Antonella, in a tone that Orinthia had not heard from her before. Her brow had darkened and the unfamiliar look of venom on her face was mystifying.

'OK, OK,' said the usher, taking a bunch of keys from her belt and riffling through them with a huff. 'But make sure they don't go wandering off anywhere.'

'Don't worry,' said Antonella curtly. 'I won't let them out of my sight.'

The usher opened up the door, and without stopping to say thank you, Orinthia and Dotty pushed their way backstage.

'Fosse! Falaise!' Orinthia called out as they made their way through a maze of corridors. They were chock-a-block with costume rails and props, the walls lined with posters of productions that had been put on in the town hall over the years.

'Come on, I think I have an idea where your cows might be,' said Antonella, reverting to her usual charming self. 'I went for a wander earlier to clear my head before competing. There are plenty of rooms downstairs. Follow me!'

She led them down a long passageway, and having made a sharp right they arrived at the top of a spiral staircase. Without hesitation Antonella made her descent, with the girls following closely behind. The stairs seemed to go on for ever, spiralling round and down, round and down. After a while, Orinthia felt so disorientated and so dizzy that it was hard to put one foot in front of the other.

But eventually they made it to the bottom, and the two girls stood doubled over, panting with exhaustion.

'So, where do you think they are?' gasped Orinthia, looking up at Antonella.

'What about in there?' the woman replied, pointing to an adjacent door with a small window. 'Why don't you go and have a look?'

'Are you sure?' said Orinthia, inching forward, puzzled. 'This looks more like the door to a storage cupboard to me. Surely Fosse and Falaise couldn't fit in—'

Orinthia's words evaporated as she felt a firm shove in her back. She stumbled forward into the door, and it swung inwards, causing her to fall knees-first into the dark room beyond. Stars danced across her field of vision, but as she tried to get up, she was pushed back down again. Soon enough, Dotty was on the floor next to her, with Antonella looming over them.

'Wh-what are you doing?' Orinthia spluttered, pain still coursing through her knees. 'You were meant to be helping us—'

'Oh, I'm sorry I gave you that impression,' said Antonella. 'But I'm afraid you've been a little too trusting.'

The woman's words hung heavy in the air and Orinthia felt the hairs lifting on the back of her neck. Something was seriously wrong and her mind reached for an explanation. 'Antonella, what's going on?'

'Game's over I'm afraid, *bambini*!' snarled the Italian woman, edging forward. She spoke quietly and slowly, making her words sound more dangerous.

Orinthia felt her stomach flip. When Mrs Gastaldini used the word *bambini* back at home, she said it affectionately and with warmth. But coming from this woman it suddenly sounded cold and threatening.

'Wh-what do you mean?' Dotty stammered. 'This isn't time to joke! We need to find our cows!'

Antonella flung back her head and laughed. 'Let's just say that they're having a nice little trip up the mountainside! I hope they're not afraid of heights.' She made the noise of a train going up the tracks and as Orinthia grasped what she was implying, she felt the blood drain from her face. *A nice little trip up the mountainside?* Did she mean that she had kidnapped Fosse and Falaise? And they were . . . on the funicular?

'No . . .' Orinthia hissed. 'They can't be! They're living, breathing animals! Why would you do such a thing? You're not going to get away with this!'

'But I already *have* got away with it,' said Antonella. 'I stopped you from competing, didn't I? Job done! So why don't you two just head back to the farmhouse and let *me* get on with winning the competition, hmm? In a few hours' time, Bruno and I will be walking out of here with the Golden Udder Award and the prize money!'

'No you won't!' shouted Orinthia. 'We'll go and tell Chief Pedersen and—'

'Oh, I don't think so,' said Antonella cruelly, leaning in so that their faces were almost touching. 'No one is going to hear you from in here! *Capito?*'

Her meaning was more than clear, but before the girls had a chance to fight back, the door was slammed shut. Plunged into near darkness, Orinthia and Dotty listened as a key was turned in the lock from the outside. Realizing that they were trapped, Orinthia began to scream, hoping that a passer-by might come to their aid. But she and Dotty had ventured far too far from the lobby and the auditorium and there was no one else down here.

Utterly powerless, the two girls listened as Antonella pounded back up the spiral staircase, leaving them completely alone.

31

'Oh my goodness, Rinthi, how did we get it so wrong?' said Dotty, slumping back against one of the walls. 'All this time we suspected Monsieur Dubois, but he was innocent all along.'

'We had plenty of reasons to think he was guilty, though,' Orinthia replied. 'No wonder we jumped to conclusions. And Antonella had been so kind to us, we had no grounds to think that she might be up to no good.'

Dotty puffed out her cheeks. 'But what are we going to do now? Mam's going to be so worried. And

Fosse and Falaise are trapped on the top of the funicular. We have to get out of here.'

Orinthia looked around, frantically searching for an escape route. They were obviously inside some kind of walk-in cleaning cupboard. Her eyes fell on a wall of shelves filled with sprays and cloths and feather dusters, but there was nothing on it that they could use to break the door down. And with no windows to escape through, they were well and truly stuck.

It was already getting uncomfortably hot. Orinthia's palms were clammy, her temperature rising. Fearing the worst, her imagination started to go into overdrive. They'd starve in here. Or die of dehydration. In hundreds of years' time, their mummified bodies would be discovered by a team of Norwegian archaeologists.

And not only that, if they didn't get out of here, what would happen to Fosse and Falaise? Two cows travelling up the mountainside in a funicular was extremely dangerous – they might hurt themselves or each other trying to escape, or cause the carriage to derail. And what if the local police got to them before they did? They might get taken to slaughter!

'Hey, hang on a minute,' said Dotty, pointing.

'What's that up there?'

Orinthia craned her neck. There was a slatted air vent above the shelves of cleaning products. Orinthia's stomach fluttered with hope. The vent was fairly small, but if they could climb up and prise it open, she was sure that they could just about squeeze through.

'We need to get up there,' she said to Dotty urgently. 'You OK with heights?'

'I guess,' said Dotty, looking up. 'But how are we going to get the vent open? There's two large screws holding it to the wall.'

Orinthia riffled through the shelves, looking for some kind of tool. But there was nothing thin and sturdy enough to loosen the screws.

'Hang on, what about this?' said Dotty, her eyes brightening as she reached into her pocket. She pulled out a wooden ice-lolly stick and handed it to Orinthia. It was sticky and stained red with strawberry juice, with a joke printed on the underside which read:

Q – WHAT DO YOU GET IF YOU PUSH A FRANKFURTER DOWN A HILL?
A – A SAUSAGE ROLL

'Dotty, I appreciate you trying to cheer me up,' said Orinthia. 'But this is no time for comedy.'

'I didn't mean for you to read the joke!' Dotty

replied. 'Although that is a funny one, I must admit. I thought that we could use the stick as a screwdriver?'

If it weren't for the fact that they were in a tiny cupboard, Orinthia would have done a victory lap on hearing her friend's idea. The ice-lolly stick was not the ideal tool for the job by any means – it was flimsy and she feared it could splinter at any moment – but it was the only tool they had, and it might just work!

'OK, I'll go up,' Orinthia said, taking the stick and popping it in her front pocket. 'You stay down here, and if you hear anyone pass by, shout as loud as you can for help.'

Dotty nodded, and taking a deep breath, Orinthia reached to the first shelf and hoisted herself up. The way it creaked under the weight of her body didn't fill her with confidence, but she couldn't lose her nerve now.

Bit by bit she ascended, releasing her increasingly sweaty palms one by one as she swung for the next shelf. She tried to breathe slowly, not daring to think about the drop if she slipped right now, nor the concrete floor that would break her fall. From such a height, she'd definitely be facing broken limbs, if not worse!

She wished more than anything that she had wings

like Geronimo or Gungho, and thoughts of the two pelicans brought tears to her eyes. She thought of all of the other creatures at the Mailbox Menagerie; of Grandy Brock and his children; of Mum, Séafra and Taber. How had she managed to get herself into yet another dangerous situation? Why had she been so reckless?

She finally made it to the top, and the air vent was within reach. She could feel cool air rushing through the slats, and she hoped with all her might that this was an indicator that their escape route would lead them outside.

'I'm going to try to loosen the screws,' she called down to Dotty.

'OK, but be careful, Rinthi,' came her worried reply. 'Take it slowly!'

Wary of losing her balance, Orinthia carefully reached into her pocket and pulled out the wooden ice-lolly stick. With a trembling hand she slotted it into the groove of the nearest screw and began to turn. It didn't come easy – the vent had obviously been attached to the wall with an electric drill and was firmly fixed into the brickwork.

But little by little the screw began to loosen, and with a few more twists of the ice-lolly stick, it fell to the floor with a satisfying high-pitched *ting!*

'Well done, Rinthi!' Dotty called up excitedly. 'Keep going, you're doing brilliantly!'

Buoyed by her friend's encouragement, Orinthia got to work on the second screw. Her makeshift tool was already starting to crack, but she couldn't let that stop her. She grasped it tight in between her fingers and turned.

'Watch your head, Dotty!' she shouted down as she twisted her wrist for the final time. 'It's coming down!'

And with that the metal vent came loose from the wall and fell to the floor with a clatter.

'Yes, Rinthi, you did it!' Dotty shouted up. 'Can you see what's on the other side?'

Orinthia peered through the oblong-shaped opening and saw that it led to an angled metal duct beyond. It was going to be a tight squeeze, but with no time to lose, she pulled herself inside and scrambled upwards. As she came to its open mouth her heart immediately leapt. She could see the sea. They were on the quayside!

32

The girls stood at the foot of the funicular, staring up the tracks. The carriage was right at the top and for a moment Orinthia half-thought about running up the mountain to get to it. But that would be foolish – it was far too steep an ascent to make on foot in the afternoon heat, especially having just made their escape from the town hall.

Orinthia looked around in panic, desperate to find someone who could help them bring the carriage back down. Surely there was an operator or machinist about?

'Excuse me!' she called out to a man passing by. 'Is there anyone on duty today? Someone working?'

The man didn't answer, and simply nodded to the nearby ticket kiosk which was attached to the funicular's engine room. Orinthia and Dotty followed his gaze, but the kiosk's shutters had been pulled down and there was nobody queuing for tickets. It was only when Dotty pointed to a sign hanging from the door bearing the words FLØIBANEN FUNICULAR – CLOSED, that Orinthia remembered that the funicular wasn't running today. It had been shut down for maintenance!

'How on earth did Antonella manage to get the carriage to the top of the tracks if the funicular is closed?' she said, running a hand through her hair.

'She must have managed to get into the engine room somehow,' said Dotty, already scouring the building for clues.

Sure enough, it wasn't long before they stumbled across a side door, its frosted glass window completely smashed in. Wasting no time, Dotty leant through it, fumbling for the door handle on the other side. But her arms weren't quite long enough and the handle was just out of reach. She pulled herself up on her tiptoes and leant over further, stretching her fingers as much as she could to try and gain purchase.

Orinthia watched with apprehension. 'Careful, Dot!' she called out. 'The smashed glass is sharp, you don't want to—'

'*Ooooooouch!*'

Dotty jolted backward, clutching her forearm to her chest. Orinthia looked down and saw that the lower sleeve of her friend's blouse had been sliced open and was blooming red with blood. As Dotty caught sight of it, the colour drained from her cheeks.

'Dot, I told you to be careful!' gasped Orinthia. 'What were you thinking?'

But now wasn't the time to argue, and Orinthia knew she had to do something to stem the bleeding. 'Dot, I'm going to need to have a look at your cut,' she said firmly, and not waiting for an answer she prized Dotty's arm away from her body. There was a huge gash across the underside of her lower arm and Orinthia couldn't help but wince. It was deep, fleshy and bleeding heavily.

'Is it bad?' asked Dotty, refusing to look.

'Well, it's not good,' said Orinthia.

Thinking fast, she suddenly remembered an entry in Ophelia Pearcart's diary where her hero been attacked by a hyena in north-east Africa, and had been forced to save her own life by using a pair of knickers to bandage a gaping wound on her thigh. She had to do something similar, and with no time to lose she kicked off her left boot and yanked off her knee-high sock. 'Don't worry, it was clean on this morning,' she reassured her friend, before binding the sock as best she could around Dotty's wound, pulling it tightly. She secured the makeshift bandage with a square knot which, while far from being naval stand-ard, seemed to do the job.

'Thanks, Rinthi,' said Dotty, breathing a sigh of relief as she pulled down her sleeve. 'Now come on, we need to get into the engine room—'

'No way, you're not going anywhere,' said Orinthia. 'Sit down here and if you feel dizzy, put your head between your knees.'

Dotty opened her mouth to protest but Orinthia was already on the move. Having seen what had happened to her friend, she didn't dare reach through the smashed glass window to get to the handle. So she lifted her boot, and with a strength she didn't know she had, kicked open the door.

Orinthia found herself in a room full of ancient-looking machinery, with a large viewing window at the far end looking up at the funicular. All she had to do was find the right button or lever, and she'd be able to bring the carriage back down the tracks. But of course, everything in the room had been labelled in Norwegian and she had no idea where to start.

'OK, let's try . . . this one,' she muttered to herself, pulling down a lever bearing the words ÅPNE DØRER towards her. She looked up at the carriage through the viewing window, and to her horror, its doors began to open! 'OK, definitely not that one!' she gasped, quickly pushing the lever back to its original position as she imagined the cows tumbling down the mountainside.

She tried another couple of buttons, but to no avail. One made the track split in two, while the other had caused an announcement to blare from a nearby tannoy.

Orinthia was beginning to give up hope.

But then she saw it.

A red button in the shape of a downwards pointing arrow.

Surely this would bring the carriage back down the tracks? She couldn't be certain of course – for all she knew this button could make the funicular carriages explode – but with no other options, she had to give it a go.

Holding her breath, she slammed her fist down on

to the button before running to the viewing window once more. She was barely able to watch, and kept her eyes half-closed as she waited to see the outcome of her decision.

She needn't have been so anxious.

All of a sudden there was a whirring from the tracks, some lights flashed at the top of the mountain, and to Orinthia's absolute relief, the carriage began to slowly descend!

She pelted back outside, and having shouted out the good news to Dotty, the two girls ran round to meet the carriage. As it approached they gasped – poor Fosse was headbutting one of the walls, and Falaise was lowing loudly with agitation.

'Don't worry, girls!' shouted Orinthia. 'Help is here!'

The carriage came to a standstill with a loud hiss, and Orinthia immediately snapped open the lock. The door swung open and the cows bounded out, mooing aggressively. They were clearly terrified, their tails flicking from side to side as they stomped around trying to get their bearings.

Not wanting to spook them any more, Orinthia proceeded towards them slowly and told Dotty to stand back.

'Easy, girls,' she said gently as they approached. 'You're OK now. Everything's fine.'

She began to gently hum a song by The Jazz Brothers of New Orleans, her soft *bee-bops* and *scabba-doo-wops* causing their ears to prick up in an instant.

They seemed to recognize her, and when she was certain that she had their trust, she reached down and offered up a couple of handfuls of grass. 'There you go,' she said as they ate. 'Is that better, hmmm?'

'How are they doing?' asked Dotty from a few metres away. 'Can I come over now?'

Orinthia nodded. 'They seem OK, but we should get them back to the town hall. It'll be good to get them checked over by a vet. You take Fosse and I'll take Falaise.'

Grasping at their reins, the girls tried to lead the two cows back down to the quayside, but they wouldn't budge. Orinthia couldn't really blame them – they'd been stuck in a tiny space atop the mountainside for hours, of course they didn't want to be told what to do. 'Come on, Falaise,' she whispered into the cow's ear. 'Easy does it—'

The sudden sound of sirens caused the girls to spin around and a car bearing the word POLITI pulled up behind them with its blue lights flashing. The back doors burst open and out bounded a worry-stricken Pem, closely followed by Herr Larsen.

'Oh my goodness!' squealed Pem, running towards the funicular and pulling Dotty into a tight squeeze. 'Where have you two been? We've been looking all over for you.'

'Ow! Mam – my arm!' Dotty replied, pulling away from her mother's grasp.

Pem shrieked as she saw the bloodied bandage. 'Dotty, are you OK? What's happened?'

'There's no time to explain, Mam. But we found Fosse and Falaise. Have they given out the Golden Udder Award yet?'

'I don't know,' said Pem, incredulously. 'But that doesn't matter now, I—'

'Pem, it really *does* matter!' Orinthia cut in. 'It was Antonella who stole Fosse and Falaise! *She's* the one who's been trying to sabotage our chances of winning!'

Pem's hands shot to her cheeks and once again Orinthia found herself stunned by the words that had come out of her mouth. After her transatlantic journey in the *Penny Black*, she never thought that she'd find herself recounting anything else as adventurous,

260

but the things that had taken place here in Bergen had been every bit as intrepid.

'Oh my goodness, this is awful,' Pem yelped. 'We need to get back to the town hall and make sure she isn't awarded the trophy and the prize money!'

Herr Larsen nodded. 'OK. You jump in the police car with the girls and get Chief Pedersen to take you back. I'll follow behind with Fosse and Falaise. We shan't let this awful woman get away with this!'

33

Orinthia felt a surge of hope flood through her as she and Dotty ran back into the town hall, with Pem and Chief Pedersen bringing up the rear. Without a moment to lose they burst into the auditorium, flinging back the double doors with a loud clatter.

But nobody noticed them. The audience was buzzing, as up on stage Mayor Rasmussen was clutching a large metallic envelope, presumably containing the name of the winning competitors. He'd obviously had an outfit change during the lunch break, and was now dressed in a sparkling silver suit with matching bow tie. Perdita Pamplemousse was by his side holding up the Golden Udder Award, which gleamed beneath the spotlight. She was still frowning despite having spent the whole day eating ice cream.

'My esteemed attendees,' the mayor began, settling the crowd. 'What a . . . erm . . . *wonderful* day we have had here in Bergen. I'd like to say that there's been many highs, but looking at the scores from the judge, it's fair to say that there have been mainly lows.' He looked at Perdita Pamplemousse and let out a nervous titter. 'Nonetheless, it is my honour to announce that the winners of this year's Golden Udder Award, with a total of four points, are . . .' He prised open the envelope and paused for dramatic effect. 'Antonella and Bruno Dolce from Italy!'

There was raucous applause from the audience, and immediately the Norwegian folk band struck up once more. Bruno and Antonella were ushered on to the stage to the sound of their national anthem, accompanied by shouts of '*Bravi!*' and '*Complimenti!*' from the Italian spectators.

'Congratulations,' said Perdita, offering up the Golden Udder. 'I don't often give out such a high score, that's for sure!'

'High score?' snapped Antonella. 'You call four out of ten a high score?' Nonetheless, she snatched the trophy from the judge's grasp and lifted it high above her head with a grin on her face. Cameras began to flash, and the audience got to their feet in ovation, whooping and cheering.

'No! Wait!' screamed Orinthia, tugging at Dotty's shirt and pulling her down the gangway towards the stage. 'She doesn't deserve that trophy! She's a cheat!'

There was a confused murmur as everyone in the auditorium turned to see what was going on, but Orinthia ignored their stares. She leapt on to the stage and snatched the microphone from the mayor's grasp. 'This woman can't win!' she shouted, planting her feet wide. 'She's lied and she's swindled! She's a complete fraudster!'

An usher appeared from the wings and tried to lead her away, but Orinthia shrugged them off, unflinching in her determination.

'What is the meaning of this?' the mayor spluttered. 'Who are you?'

'I'm part of the British team,' said Orinthia. 'The ones who had to pull out.' She shot Antonella the darkest of glares. 'And it was because of this woman.

She wanted to sabotage our chance of winning so she stole our ice cream and our cows!'

Perdita Pamplemousse guffawed. 'What on earth are you talking about? Stole your *cows*? Is this some kind of joke?'

'Of . . . of course it is,' stuttered Antonella, trying to feign ignorance. 'I have no idea who this girl is or what she's talking about.' She turned to Mayor Rasmussen and batted her eyelashes. 'Now, my son and I have a flight back home to Italy in a few hours, so can we please get on with the ceremony, hmm? Where's my cash prize?'

'No!' Orinthia shouted, baring her teeth. 'You're a criminal and we can prove it!'

She waved to the doorway, and within a moment Herr Larsen came bounding forth with Fosse and Falaise.

'We brought these cows all the way from England,' said Dotty, joining Orinthia on stage. 'They were going to be part of our presentation today. We'd trained them to present our ice cream cones to Perdita Pamplemousse.'

'W-w-what?' gasped Antonella. 'I've never seen these animals in my life!'

'It's OK,' the mayor reassured, patting the Italian

woman's arm. 'These girls are obviously just mistaken—'

But just then a man in the audience stood up. 'Hang on a minute, I knew I recognized you from somewhere!' He edged towards the stage and jabbed an accusing finger at Antonella. 'You were trying to sell me those cows at the cattle auction yesterday – said they were good for the slaughter. I knew straight away that you were lying, of course. These are obviously dairy cows, not beef cows.'

Orinthia couldn't believe what she was hearing. 'So not only did you steal Fosse and Falaise, but you were trying to destroy the evidence by getting them turned into fillet steak?' she shrieked.

'Nonsense!' said Antonella, making a last-ditch attempt to save her skin. 'These girls are obviously just jealous because *I* won the award.'

Orinthia felt her blood boiling. 'Jealous? We're not the ones who resorted to threats, to theft, to kidnap! You knew your own ice cream wasn't good enough to win the competition so all you could do was cheat!' She lunged towards the Italian woman, knocking the trophy from her grasp. 'You don't deserve that!'

'Security! Security!' said the mayor, looking around desperately for backup. 'Someone needs to escort these children and their livestock from the building *immediately*!' He clicked his fingers and two burly men dashed to his rescue. All Dotty and Orinthia could do was watch as they came lolloping towards them, clicking their knuckles.

'No! Wait, Mayor Rasmussen!' shouted Chief Pedersen, before throwing himself in front of the security guards. 'The girls are not lying. I found them at the bottom of the mountain just fifteen minutes ago. They'd rescued the cows from the funicular!' He wheeled round to face Antonella, his lips curling. 'This woman had locked them in one of the carriages and they'd been stuck at the top of the mountain all day!'

There was a loud gasp of incredulity from the audience.

'Cows in a funicular?' laughed Antonella nervously. 'Whatever are these crazy people going to accuse me of next? And besides, the funicular was closed for maintenance today. How could I possibly have had access to the carriages?'

'Because you got into the engine house and tampered with the controls!' Dotty shrieked. She pulled up her sleeve to reveal her bloodied, bandaged arm. 'Look – I cut myself on the window she smashed when she broke in!'

There was a crash as someone in the audience fainted, and Antonella looked to the floor sheepishly. Every person in every seat had their eyes set firmly on her, and the Italian woman obviously knew that the game was up. 'Well, I think it's time for us to be going,' she said, shuffling backwards towards the wings with Bruno in tow. The poor boy looked terrified. 'Like I said, we have a flight to catch—'

'Oh, I don't think so!' came a sudden shout from the back of the auditorium. '*Non vai da nessuna parte!*'

Shielding her eyes from the spotlight, Orinthia looked up over the audience. A bowler-hatted man dressed in a suit was standing up in the back row, brandishing a walking cane.

Orinthia gasped as she realized who it was. 'Monsieur Dubois?'

'No, *bambina*, not Monsieur Dubois.'

The man shuffled into the gangway and slowly made his way towards the stage. Dropping his cane, he looked up at Orinthia. Then with a deep breath he took off his hat, which, much to everyone's surprise, had a wig attached to it. He removed his glasses next, before starting to peel away his facial hair. Beneath the disguise was the face of an old woman.

A loud gasp rang around the auditorium like a fork striking a glass, and Orinthia dropped to her knees. Standing before them was Mrs Gastaldini.

34

'Mrs Gastaldini, what . . . what's going on?' stuttered Orinthia, her mouth dry. 'Is this some kind of joke? Why were you dressed up as Monsieur Dubois?'

Mrs Gastaldini edged closer to the stage, loosening her shirt and tie as she tried to catch her breath. 'I'm so sorry, *bambini*,' she wheezed. 'I know this must have come as quite a shock but I can explain. I-I—'

'Serafina, be quiet!' Antonella hissed, appearing from the wings and running to the front of the stage. Her nostrils were flaring, her eyes fixed on Mrs

Gastaldini. '*Stai zitta!*'

Orinthia balked. Had she heard correctly? Had Antonella just called Mrs Gastaldini by her first name? Did they . . . know each other? 'Have you two met before?' she asked Mrs Gastaldini, already fearing the answer.

The old woman ran a hand through her hair, sighing heavily. It was as if she had the weight of the world pressing down on her shoulders. 'It pains me to say it, Orinthia, and I don't expect you to forgive me, but Antonella is . . . my niece.'

Orinthia's mouth slackened and she spluttered. Not only did Mrs Gastaldini know this criminal, but they were family? Surely it couldn't be true?

'I don't believe this!' shouted Dotty. '*You* were part of this all along? You wanted us to lose today too?'

'No!' protested Mrs Gastaldini, turning her gaze to Orinthia. 'It's not like that! Please, *bambina*, let me explain!'

Orinthia nodded, not knowing what else to say or do. 'Go on.'

Mrs Gastaldini continued. 'We've always been close and Antonella always loved hearing about my life in Little Penhallow. England is very different to *Italia* after all.

271

'But when I told her about Dotty and her mums' plans to enter the Golden Udder Awards, she started asking a lot of questions. Of course, I was delighted at first. I even thought that she and Bruno could come and visit the *Penny Lick*. I'd done nothing but praise Dotty and her mums' *gelato*.

'But then Antonella decided that she wanted to enter the competition too. It turns out that the family ice cream business hasn't been doing as well as I thought, and she said that the prize money would help her fix things.' She took a deep breath. 'That's when she started threatening me. She said that I needed to stop the Ambroses from entering to help her win. She said that my loyalties should be with her own flesh and blood.'

Up on stage, Antonella lunged forwards. 'Serafina, *zietta*, you don't have to do this!' she hissed. 'I'm not going to be the only one in trouble if you keep on talking, *capito*?'

Mrs Gastaldini turned to the stage. 'I'm willing to face the consequences. This has gone on long enough and these poor girls have been through too much already.'

For a while, Orinthia stood deep in thought. Suddenly everything that had gone on over the past few weeks started slotting together in her mind like pieces of a jigsaw puzzle. 'So it was *you* who left that threatening note in the ballot box?' she asked Mrs Gastaldini. '*You* fed the ice cream to Fosse and Falaise to make them sick? *You* took the batteries out of Grandy Brock's alarm clock the morning we were due to leave for London?'

'I'm so sorry,' sniffled Mrs Gastaldini. 'I didn't want to, you have to believe me. But . . . but I felt torn. Two Scoops Creamery is already such a huge success, and I convinced myself that maybe Antonella needed the prize money more. I tried to talk to her, but she said that our family back in Italy would never forgive me if I didn't do as she said.'

There was silence for a moment, every audience member on every chair trying to process the words that had just been spoken.

'So the day that Zuni got into the creamery,' Dotty jumped in. 'You were there too, weren't you?'

Mrs Gastaldini nodded forlornly. 'I followed you there and she flew inside. What an old fool I am. I couldn't even spy on you without causing a huge scene.'

Orinthia swallowed, trying to take everything in. 'And your brother, is he *actually* ill?'

'That was just part of the act too,' said Mrs Gastaldini, hanging her head in shame. 'After everything I'd done, I needed an excuse to go back to Napoli. I couldn't bear the thought of staying in Little Penhallow, living with all that guilt. I didn't want to lie any more.'

'So you weren't ever going to come back to Tupenny Mill? You just left without telling anyone?' Orinthia felt a bolt of fury. 'What about Grandy Brock?'

On hearing his name, Mrs Gastaldini blushed. 'He's why I'm here now. I'd packed my bags to go to Italy and was on my way to the train station when I had a change of heart. I knew that running away wasn't the right thing to do. And that's why I followed you to the port and got on board the *Mollusca*. I knew I needed to keep an eye on you and Dotty in Norway, to make sure that Antonella didn't do anything to harm you. So I disguised myself as Monsieur Dubois.'

The magnitude of the revelation shook Orinthia to the core and she stumbled backwards, unable to speak.

Mrs Gastaldini shook her head gravely. 'I'm so sorry. I just hope that one day you, Dotty and Pem can forgive me . . .'

With nothing more to say, the old woman took a

seat in the empty chair at the end of the front row, and let her face fall into her hands.

Orinthia didn't know what to think. Her head was swirling with anger and disappointment and confusion. What Mrs Gastaldini had done was terrible, *really* terrible, but her niece had put her in an impossible situation – family loyalty was a powerful thing, after all. But then again, what about Mrs Gastaldini's loyalty to Grandy Brock and his children? They had welcomed her into their lives, their home, with open arms. She'd practically been living with them at Tupenny Mill.

Mrs Gastaldini looked up, her eyes red. 'Orinthia, please say something. I'll understand if you never want to see me again, but just speak to me.'

'It's OK, Rinthi,' said Pem softly, looking up to Orinthia with trembling hands. 'You don't have to talk if you don't want to.'

Orinthia sighed, letting her thoughts stew. She felt so betrayed, so hurt, but she knew that everyone made mistakes – she'd made plenty herself in the past year, after all. Under the unflinching gaze of the hushed audience she got down from the stage and knelt down by Mrs Gastaldini. 'It's OK,' she whispered, her hand hovering over her shoulder as if to comfort her. 'You did what you thought you had to and—'

'Rinthi, are you mad? What are you doing?' shouted Dotty suddenly from up on stage. 'We don't even know if she's telling the truth. This is probably just some elaborate story to save her own skin. She just wants Antonella to take all of the blame for what's gone on!'

'No, don't say that!' protested Mrs Gastaldini. '*Non sto mentendo!* I'm not lying!' She looked up to her niece and held out her hands in plea. 'Antonella, admit to what you've done,' she begged. 'These children have to know the truth.'

For a moment there was silence, and Orinthia prayed that Antonella was going to come clean.

But she was on the move in a flash.

Grabbing Bruno's wrist with one hand, she swept up the trophy with the other, jumped from the stage, and pelted up the aisle in the direction of the exits. She was going to get away!

But Fosse and Falaise had other plans.

The two cows had begun to paw angrily in the gangway, their nostrils flared and their tails raised in alarm. Their heads shook violently, and Orinthia knew exactly what they were planning – they were about to charge!

In an instant they too were pelting towards the exits, and as their horns made contact with Antonella's bottom, she was thrown up into the air.

'*Mama miaaaaa! Che vacca cattiva!*' she yelped, landing back on the ground with a heavy *thump*. She rolled around, doubled up in pain, pleading to the cows for mercy. 'Please, please don't hurt me, *vacca!*' she yelped. 'I'll never eat steak again, I promise!'

Orinthia strode forward, standing over the sorry-looking woman with venom and pain and hurt in her eyes. 'Admit to what you've done or I'll order the cows to strike again,' she ordered, crossing her arms.

'OK, OK, I admit it,' whimpered Antonella, looking rightly petrified. 'I threatened my aunt then stole your ice cream and your cows. I'm sorry. But please let me go, I'll never enter the Golden Udder Awards ever again.'

'Too right you won't!' bellowed Perdita Pamplemousse, hobbling down from the stage. 'You awful, awful cheat! And to think that I gave you such a high score!'

Orinthia hadn't thought that the judge's face could get any grumpier-looking than it already had, but she was wrong. With nostrils flaring and teeth bared, the tiny woman came storming up the gangway and snatched the trophy from Antonella's grasp. 'I'll be taking that, thank you very much!'

There was the sound of jangling metal as Chief Pedersen stepped forward holding a pair of handcuffs. He shook them defiantly in Antonella's face, causing her to snarl with rage. 'Antonella Dolce, I'm arresting you on suspicion of theft, kidnap, fraud . . . and no doubt lots of other awful things too. I shall be taking you into custody immediately.'

35

Up on stage, the mayor coughed. 'Well, in light of recent events, I guess it is only just that the Golden Udder Award should be given to the competitor with the next highest score . . .' He ran a finger down the sheet of paper on his clipboard. 'And that means that the winner of this year's trophy is Yoshimitsu Mori from Japan with his green-tea ice cream! Could Mr Mori and his team please make their way to the stage?'

There was a polite ripple of applause from the crowd, but it was obvious that most people in the audience were now past caring about the competition.

'Hang on a minute!' interrupted Perdita Pample-mousse. 'What about the British competitors? Surely I should try their ice cream first? Especially now that they have their cows back.'

Mayor Rasmussen looked shocked at her sudden display of compassion. 'Well, of course, Perdita. If you don't mind sparing more of your precious time?'

'To be honest, getting the chance to try the Ambroses' ice cream was the only reason I agreed to be judge here today. I've heard so many good things about it.'

Orinthia couldn't believe what she was hearing. Did this grumpy old lady, the one that had been so negative about the day's proceedings, really just say that she was eager to try their ice cream? It was such a shame that Helios hadn't arrived in time.

'As much as we appreciate your kind offer, Ms Pamplemousse, I'm afraid we'll have to decline,' she uttered. 'After Antonella stole our ice cream we tried to get some more sent over from England, but unfortunately it didn't arrive. We didn't want to make anything else in a rush, as we felt it would be below standard.'

'Well, that is a shame,' Perdita Pamplemousse

replied. 'Although I appreciate your commitment to perfection. A girl after my own heart.' Her trademark scowl returned once more as she looked out across the audience with accusing eyes. 'Many of the competitors here should take note, in fact!'

Pem smiled bashfully. 'We'll be back next year with a vengeance though, mark my word—'

The door to the auditorium was flung open once more, and in dashed a man, red-cheeked and breathless. It was one of the ushers, and he was chasing a large-winged creature who was zooming down the aisle towards the stage. 'Come back here!' he shouted, swiping through the air with little success. 'Come back here!'

Orinthia and Dotty stole a look upwards and gasped.

'It's Helios!' shouted Orinthia, noticing the little cool bag hanging from the bird's beak. 'And he has our ice cream!' She held out a hand, and the feathered creature came to rest on it, obviously exhausted after his journey. Opening up the cool bag, it wasn't a surprise to find that the ice cream had almost melted, but Orinthia knew it would still taste good. 'Ms Pamplemousse,' she said, turning back towards the judge. 'If the offer still stands, we *would* like you to sample our ice cream after all.'

'It would be my pleasure,' the Norwegian woman said with a smile. And with that, she took the silver sampling spoon from her bag and plunged it into the tub of melty pink cream that Orinthia had offered up. She slurped up a mouthful noisily, and sloshed it around her mouth.

'Well?' asked Mayor Rasmussen, his impatience mirroring that of Dotty, Orinthia and Pem.

Perdita Pamplemousse was licking her lips. 'I'm getting raspberry . . . suet pudding . . . cream . . . and is that a hint of nutmeg I detect?'

'Yes,' Pem replied timidly, grasping Dotty's hand. 'Do you like it? Is it good?'

'No, I don't think it's very good, actually . . .' said the judge, causing Orinthia's heart to temporarily sink. 'I think it's . . . absolutely fantastic! Obviously I cannot give it full marks, as its consistency is, well . . . a little soft. But on flavour alone, I would easily give it seven points!'

The mayor smiled. 'In which case I think we have our winners. The recipients of this year's trophy and prize money are . . . Two Scoops Creamery from Great Britain! Let's give our *new* champions a huge round of applause.'

The crowd erupted, and Dotty, Orinthia and Pem threw their arms around each other with glee. They began to jump around in circles, whooping and wailing at the top of their lungs.

They'd done it! They were taking home the Golden Udder Award!

36

'Come and try our new ice cream flavour!' Dotty shouted from the serving hatch of the *Penny Lick*. 'Jam roly-poly pudding! Get it while you can!'

Pandora appeared at her side, beaming with pride. 'That's right, come and get your award-winning ice cream! Freshly churned today!'

There was no real need for them to try and drum up business – a huge crowd of people had already gathered on the village green, all waiting to get a taste of Two Scoops Creamery's new offering.

Orinthia, Séafra, Taber and the Brock children

had joined the queue in an instant, their chatter quickly turning to strawberry sauce and chopped nuts and chocolate flakes.

It had been a few days since the Golden Udder Award winners had returned from Norway and things were slowly getting back to normal. Séafra had spent the time listening to his sister's tales of cow-kidnap, theft and funiculars, and Taber, finally free from chickenpox, was back to his usual energetic self. Mum, at first angry that her daughter had got herself into yet another dangerous situation, was now just glad to have Orinthia home safe and well.

Despite everything that had happened with her niece, Mrs Gastaldini had been welcomed back to Tupenny Mill with open arms, and the Brock children were delighted to have her back in charge of the kitchen! 'Grandy Brock should never be allowed near parsnips ever again,' Kipling had lamented.

Saying goodbye to Bergen had been sad, but Herr Larsen had already invited Orinthia and Dotty to join him for a week of cross-country skiing during the winter holidays. He'd also urged the girls to take some jars of pickled herring to enjoy back at home, but they'd politely and gracefully declined. That was one thing about Norway that they definitely weren't going to miss!

Hearing her name being called from the shade of a nearby oak tree, Orinthia turned from her spot in the queue. Mum was perched on a gingham blanket laid with crockery, napkins and cutlery, and was carefully pulling Tupperware containers of food out of a large wicker picnic basket. Hand in hand, Grandy Brock and Mrs Gastaldini were sipping on glasses of fresh lemonade, and Farmer Newing and Pem were feeding apples to Fosse and Falaise, who were reclining beneath the hedgerow.

'Come on you lot, lunch is ready,' called Mum. 'Come and sit.'

'Don't worry about lunch, Mum, we're having ice cream!' Orinthia yelled back.

'No you are not, Orinthia Shalloo! There'll be plenty of time for ice cream later. And besides, I thought you'd be sick of the stuff by now.'

'Never!' said Orinthia with a chuckle. And dragging herself away from the queue, she headed across the green with her friends and brothers in tow.

The picnic was a sight to behold. At its centre was a huge platter of sandwiches, cut into delicate triangles with their crusts removed. Other plates and dishes surrounded it, laden with minted new potatoes, sliced ham, pats of butter, cheeses, sausage rolls and jam tarts. And that wasn't all – Orinthia couldn't believe her eyes when Mrs Gastaldini opened yet another wicker picnic basket, and proceeded to unpack even more tasty morsels, including a majestic apple tart sprinkled with sugar.

'OK, everyone, tuck in!' said Mum, gesturing for everyone to help themselves. 'I hope I've made enough!'

'Of course you have,' said Grandy Brock, reaching out with a reassuring hand. 'As always, you have been the most generous of hosts.'

'What fillings are in the sandwiches?' asked Orinthia, leaning over and inspecting what was on offer.

'Ha! What fillings *aren't* there more like!' said Mrs Gastaldini. 'Your mother and I have been slicing bread all morning! There's egg and cress . . . roast beef with mustard . . . smoked salmon and cucumber . . . coronation chicken and . . .' She pointed to the white-bread sandwiches with a generous filling. 'Those ones are *formaggio e pomodoro*! Your favourite!'

'Oooh yummy!' said Orinthia, grabbing as many of the latter as she could fit on her plate.

Food was passed between the children at speed, and soon not a single centimetre of empty plate could be seen. They ate noisily and with gusto, and there wasn't much difference between the sound they made while gobbling down their lunch and that of Fosse and Falaise chewing the cud!

'So, what was the farm in the mountains like?' asked Kipling, reaching for an iced bun.

'It was so beautiful, Kip,' said Dotty. 'The scenery, the fresh air, the fjords. I think you'd really like it.'

'And what about the RMS *Mollusca*?' pressed Suki, who was sitting with Caspian snuggled up on her lap. 'Was it good to see Mog again, Rinthi?'

Orinthia beamed. 'It was brilliant. We got to have a first-class cabin *and* try Pineapple Royale. Mog says a big hello to everyone, and he's hoping to come visit again soon – when Captain Binnacle gives him a day off!'

These were the first of many more questions, and it took the best part of the afternoon for all of the details of the girls' Norwegian adventure (both good *and* bad) to be recounted.

'I'm so sorry to hear about what you had to go through with your niece, Serafina,' said Mum to Mrs Gastaldini, patting her on the arm. 'What a rotter!'

Mrs Gastaldini nodded mournfully. 'Yes, it was all very sad. But Antonella *has* written to apologize. It will take a while to rebuild our relationship, of course, but I'd like to be able to forgive her one day.'

Mum smiled. 'And in the meantime you know you have all of us. Me and my three. Suki, Bramwell, Kipling, Peggy, Caspian . . .'

'And you have me too, of course,' said Grandy Brock softly, and with that he leant over and planted a huge kiss right on Mrs Gastaldini's lips.

There was a moment of stunned silence before everyone broke into cheers, followed by the obligatory *stwit-stwoos* from the younger children.

Kipling, as if witnessing the balcony scene in *Romeo and Juliet*, wrung his hands together with glee. 'Finally!' he swooned. 'Love is in the air!'

At the same time, Pandora came rushing across the green towards them. 'Hey, everyone! You'll be pleased to hear that the *Penny Lick* has already sold out of the jam roly-poly ice cream. Dotty, Pem, you're going to have to start churning some more!'

'*After* lunch!' said Pem, pouring her wife a glass of lemonade. 'Now, come and join us. There's still plenty of food left.'

'Here, have my spot,' said Farmer Newing, getting up and offering Pandora a seat. 'As much as I'd like to stay, I have to head back to the farm.' He meandered over to Fosse and Falaise and picked up their reins. 'Need to be getting these two bedded down. This heat is getting too much for them I fear. Come on, ladies . . .'

But as much as Farmer Newing tried to pull them away, the cows wouldn't budge. He tried giving them a nudge from behind, then bribing them with a couple of sandwiches, but it was no use!

'It seems as though they are more than happy here with you lot,' he said. 'Not sure what to do, really. Ever since coming back from Norway they've seemed more content in your company than mine. Fickle old things!'

'I have a suggestion,' said Pandora, sitting down, before turning to Pem. 'If my wife agrees with me, of course.'

Farmer Newing scratched his head. 'Go on.'

'Well, what with Fosse and Falaise being so well trained now, it would be a shame for their talents to go to waste. What if Two Scoops Creamery were to buy them from you? Then they could deliver ice creams for us around the village. A new strand of the business!'

Dotty gasped in delight. 'Oh Mum, that's an amazing idea! Mam, what do you think? Can we take on Fosse and Falaise?'

Pem swallowed down a mouthful of chocolate éclair and smiled. 'Of course we can,' she said, her voice clotted with cream and pastry. 'I couldn't think of better business partners. As long as Fosse and Falaise don't mind wearing hair nets! Or should that be *fur* nets?'

Everyone laughed.

'And I know exactly what we can call this exciting new strand of your business,' said Orinthia, looking rather pleased with herself. 'The Sundae Delivery Service.'

Acknowledgements

I'm surrounded by so many wonderful people in my life, and as each year passes there seem to be more and more of you to thank – I'm an incredibly lucky girl to have such a beautiful support network of family, friends and colleagues.

Firstly, I want to thank everyone at Chicken House for taking me under your wing and championing my writing: Barry, Rachel L, Rachel H, Laura M, Laura S, Jazz, Olivia, Emily, Elinor and Esther. And the hugest thanks to my editor Kesia Lupo; I will miss you and your ugly 1990s sweatshirts – but our loss is the USA's gain!

Next, to my agent Kate Shaw. Thank you for emails, texts and chats full of wisdom. I always feel buoyed and optimistic after speaking to you.

I have a huge family and love you all very much – Mum and Graeme; Dad and Mary; Manda and Glen; Poppy and Tots; Beth; Luke and Dee; Nick and Kate; Marky; Judith; Pat; Grandma; Mamgu. Jacko – you are both a brilliant brother and a brilliant mate – thanks for understanding me, always.

And now to my friends, comrades and confidantes! Freddy – thank you for understanding, compassion and memories. To my Cackles Coven for twenty-five years of magical times. To the Hay on Wye Weekenders for being there through the good, the bad and the embarrassing – we are forever twelve-and-a-half! To CLaN CIC for beautiful days and nights under canvas. Continued thanks to The Golden Egg Academy and to all my fellow writers for supporting me on this journey. Katy, for always being there. Kelly and Nick, Holly and Pom – I long for the day that we'll all be in the same country again. Poppy and Tom, for making your home a place I want to visit every week. Andy and Andrew, for our writing/port-drinking sessions. Baker, thank you for being a buddy and a champion of my work. Gabi – once again, huge hugs for ensuring I can pay my bills each month (and sorry for not always switching on the lights!). And to 27 – you are a sweater vest of honesty, joy and happy times.

A huge shout-out to my drama and creative writing students; you're noisy and chaotic and imaginative and fearless and brave – everything that children should be. I want to give a special mention to Lemi for her thought-provoking feedback and for giving Milky his 'forever' name – you are the most enlightening of young women. To Toby, for your infectious enthusiasm and love of reading. And to Pip – thank you for giving me the idea for the Greek Salad Sundae – you're an incredible writer and I just know we'll all be reading *your* books one day very soon.

Big *cwtches* to all the other little sproglets I get to hang out with – Romilly, Indigo and Florence; Otis; Olive; Hazel and Gwilym; Minerva; Luca and Zeno; Alice; Úna; Noah and Thea; Gwen and Mabli; Lyra – I write these adventures with all of your cheeky faces in mind.

And to you lovely lot – my readers – thanks for sticking with my books. I hope you enjoy my stories as much as I love writing them.

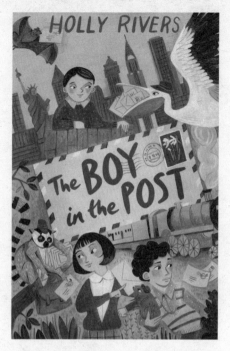

THE BOY IN THE POST

The Shalloo children are spending their summer holidays helping elderly expostman, Grandy Brock, set up an extraordinary new postal service staffed by furry and feathered posties.

Orinthia, Séafra and Taber are especially fond of top recruits Geronimo and Gungho – pelicans with exceptional inner compasses. But when one of the big birds fails to return from an important delivery, the children are afraid something awful has happened. Determined to find out, the youngest Shalloo, Taber, with the help of a fancy stamp, posts himself to the New York zipcode where Geronimo was sent. When the other children discover what their brother has done, they follow suit, and soon all are embarked on the most amazing, first-class adventure by land, sea and sky.

Paperback, ISBN 978-1-912626-04-5, £7.99 • ebook, ISBN 978-1-913696-54-2, £7.99